Pride Publishing books by J. B. Knowles

Oathtaker
Broken

I0670706

Oathtaker

BROKEN

J. B. KNOWLES

Broken
ISBN # 978-1-80250-520-7
©Copyright J. B. Knowles 2023
Cover Art by Kelly Martin ©Copyright February 2023
Interior text design by Claire Siemaszkiewicz
Pride Publishing

Published in 2023 by Pride Publishing, United Kingdom.

Pride Publishing is an imprint of Totally Entwined Group Limited.

BROKEN

Dedication

To Cathy, Jack and Brady. You're still my heroes.

Prologue

Twenty years before Day Zero

Even without the blindfold, there would have been very little to see. The forest around Katya and Shira was completely unlit.

Not that being blindfolded bothered Katya much — elves had excellent hearing and balance. Between the two, she had very little trouble navigating the winding path.

"We're almost there, girl." The ranger's voice was clear but hushed.

"Good. I'm ready to get at this."

"Calm yourself, Katya." Shira's voice held a touch of reproach. "I know you've thought long and hard about this evening and what it means, but the Council needs to see you measured and in control."

Katya took a deep breath and slowly exhaled. "Yes, you're right. I'm just anxious."

"I understand that. I was the same way." Katya could hear the humour and warm memories in his voice.

After another dozen steps, Shira's grip on her arm brought her to a stop.

"In a few seconds, you can take the blindfold off and I'll be leaving you on your own to join the Council ranks. Listen to the directions from the Three and remember what we talked about. Everything will be fine. And remember, it's tradition that new Oathtakers buy the first round."

Katya smiled. "There's a tab already opened at the Scary Salmon. If you fail to plan…"

"…you plan to fail, yes." The ranger's tone was dry. "I seem to recall mentioning that to you once or twice." His hand left her arm. "I'm off, Katya. Good luck. You've sacrificed much to get here tonight. I'm very proud of you."

His footsteps crunched away into the forest.

Katya was pleasantly surprised. "Proud" was not a word her mentor used lightly, and it drove home to her how important this ceremony was.

She removed the black cloth, counting to ten before opening her eyes so her excellent night vision wouldn't be overwhelmed by the light that she knew was now surrounding her.

Even though she knew what to expect, she was still surprised.

She was standing on the edge of a large clearing. At its middle was a massive fire burning in a wide pit. Figures of various shapes and sizes stood silent, hoods hiding their specific race or gender.

Katya could, however, make some educated guesses as to who or what was shadowed beneath some of the cloaks. She recognised the short stature of a greyling and the massive sloping shoulders of a cave giant. She glimpsed a long, muscular tail coiled on the ground behind one figure, marking it as a member of the scaly naga race. A few spots down from the naga, Katya noticed the tips of treelike branches sticking out from under a hood that didn't quite cover all of a spriggan's head.

Regardless of who they were, each held a long staff tipped with flame. After watching the unusual light dance for a few seconds, Katya realised her initial guess that it was flame was wrong. Whatever it was flickered like fire, but burned a bright scarlet red, casting deep shadows onto the trees around the clearing.

She walked through an opening in the circle of figures. When she had gone two steps inside the ring, a solemn voice said, "Stop."

She did.

Three individuals sat on large stone chairs near the roaring fire. Unlike the rest, they were not hooded. They were the Three — senior members of the Council of the Blood Oath. At least one of them had personally inducted every new Oathtaker for almost the last century.

From what Katya could see, two were human. The other appeared to be some type of feline. It was difficult to tell as the Three were silhouetted against the fire, but the pointed ears and what appeared to be a fuzzy coating of short fur were good enough for a guess.

"You are Katya Greenleaf." It was an affirmation, not a question.

"Yes."

"You come here tonight of your own free will." Again, Katya was being tested, not questioned.

"Yes."

There was a pause.

"Katya Greenleaf, you come before the Council this night to take the Blood Oath. It is not an obligation to be undertaken lightly. Once you become an Oathtaker, you join a lineage of warriors who have forsworn all other pursuits except the hunting and extermination of those who would bring evil to this world and others. Those who bear the Mark of the Oath designate themselves as an enemy of chaos and a target for all who know of the Council and its mission."

There was another pause, presumably to let Katya digest this.

"Katya Greenleaf, do you still undertake to join our ranks?"

Katya took a deep breath. "I do."

"Very well." The central person of the Three turned and nodded his head to a hooded figure standing to the side of the stone chairs, separate from the rest, who moved to stand in front of Katya.

"Your arm." It was a female voice.

Katya understood what was coming. She slid her right sleeve up and presented her forearm, palm up.

The figure removed what Katya knew to be a brand from under her robe. At a whispered command, the head of the brand began to glow with the same crimson light topping the torches around the fire.

Without a word, the brand was placed onto the smooth skin on Katya's wrist. She inhaled strongly in surprise. While she was expecting a burn, like hot metal or wood, the touch was in fact shockingly cold, like frostbite.

It didn't last long and after a few seconds, Katya peered at her wrist. By the light of the fire, she could just make out a series of red lines, some solid, some broken. The Mark of the Oathtakers.

"Katya Greenleaf." The middle of the Three had spoken again and she turned back into the circle.

"You have made a momentous decision tonight. The elves are a noble race and we are pleased that we now have one among our number again."

Katya smiled. It was no shock to hear that she was the sole elven member of the Oathtakers. Being an anomaly was nothing new for her.

"The next time this Council convenes, you will be among your brothers and sisters of the circle. We wish you safe travels and swift justice."

The Three stood. As they did, the gathered members of the Council bowed their heads. Katya, feeling the power of the evening and of the brotherhood she had joined, bowed hers as well.

The Three turned and moved into the darkness surrounding the ring of torches. As soon as they moved past the crimson light, the night swallowed them up.

The member who had branded her pulled off her hood. To Katya's surprise, a beautiful human with long dark hair and what Katya would come to discover were deep brown eyes was revealed. She smiled, giving Katya a slight flutter in her stomach that she knew had nothing to do with receiving her Mark.

With a tone of reproach, the voice in her head reminded her that this was not an appropriate time to be contemplating companionship of that sort and that she needed to focus. Katya knew the voice was right, but there were times she wished it would stay quiet more often.

It wasn't a real voice, of course. Katya considered it to be the part of her that exercised common sense, that asked questions she knew she should stop avoiding, that tried to calm her when she knew her emotions were beginning to get the better of her.

She occasionally had full conversations with herself this way, weighing the pros and cons of different situations. Sometimes she listened to the voice... sometimes she ignored it. It was a very methodical way of working things out.

The brunette held out her right hand. Katya met it with her own, placing her palm against the Mark on the other woman's arm. The warrior's grip, it was called.

"I'm Amrada. Welcome to the family."

Katya returned her smile. "Thank you."

Behind Amrada, Katya saw other members of the Council removing their own hoods and moving to congratulate her...humans of all types, dwarves. As she had guessed, a greyling, a giant, a naga and a spriggan were among the group. There were even a few assorted races Katya didn't recognise.

Shira moved through the crowd now surrounding Katya. He made it to her and extended his hand. She returned his grip, holding it a bit longer than normal in deference to his role as her mentor.

The old ranger smiled. "I'm glad you went through with it. I've seen more than one person back out at the last minute."

She laughed. "Did you think I'd do the same?"

The smile widened to a grin. "Not for a moment."

Shira looked around at the crowd. "Brothers and sisters. Tonight, we welcome a new sister to the fold." He paused for a few cheers.

"As is tradition, our new Oathtaker will treat us all to a cold drink to quench the fire of her welcome."

The cheers were considerably louder this time.

"To the tavern!"

With a final cheer, the assemblage moved out of the clearing, heading for the small town in the distance, and the mugs and goblets waiting there.

Amrada held her arm out to Katya. "Shall we join them?"

Bemused, Katya linked her arm with Amrada's. "Yes. Without delay."

As they walked, with Amrada chatting about what awaited Katya as an Oathtaker, the elf pondered her new purpose, her new mission and her new life. For the first time in many years, she felt as if she had found a place where she belonged.

Chapter One

Day Zero

The swamp went against everything Katya had ever learned about choosing a battlefield.

She stood in freezing knee-high water surrounded by small islands of reed-covered sand. Thick mist hung in the air, limiting her vision and rendering her favoured weapon, a crossbow, useless.

The fog was freezing and damp, and despite the enchantments on the leather armour she wore, a chill was creeping into her bones. In that, Katya wasn't alone. The other members of her party were also complaining about the wet and frosty surroundings.

The swirling mist made sounds duller and flatter, but with her better-than-human hearing, Katya could hear the clicks and whistles that made up the language of the lizard men that were closing in on them. They were savage and bloodthirsty creatures, given to torture and enslaving defeated enemies, fighting to the last with massive clubs of wood and jagged stone axes.

Today it was Katya's job to lead the fight against this party of lizard men, sending a message from local merchants and crafters' guilds that it was time the lizards put a halt to their destruction of trade missions and killing of travelling merchants passing through the area, and that their immediate departure from the swamp would be appreciated.

The responsibility weighed on Katya, despite her eagerness to mix it up, and because of this, she was not happy with what was going to be a horrible place for a stand-up fight.

Still, neither weather nor terrain mattered to Katya. Oathtakers didn't just head into battle when the skies were sunny and pleasant. Dead enemies were dead no matter where their bodies ended up.

The mist beside her parted and Shira appeared, his beard caked with frost. Katya knew her own long hair looked the same, even though she wore it tied back. Function over form was the warrior's way.

The old ranger gestured with his chin towards the swamp.

"Ugly spot."

"I've seen worse. That garbage pit on the coast? Blah."

Shira laughed. "I'll never forget that smell. Nor the rats."

Katya suppressed the shudder that rolled up her back. *Gods, the rats,* she remembered. Vile and voracious monsters that had wiped out all the wild animals in a huge area around the garbage dump. When they had moved on to livestock, the farmers in the area were desperate for help. The Oathtakers had answered the call.

The rats had been the same size as large dogs, with yellow eyes and even yellower teeth — one of them had bitten straight through a party member's leather gauntlet. When all was said and done, everyone in the fray had ended up with scratches and bites from the filthy beasts that needed to be well-cleaned before infection set in.

Their foul bloodstains never had come off Katya's armour completely, no matter how often she scrubbed them.

"I think the lizards will give them a run for their money today."

Shira's face took on the more serious look that Katya was accustomed to — his war-face. "They may, aye. What did our friend in the sky say?"

Katya looked up, straining to see. "I haven't talked to her yet. Do you want me to call her in?"

"May as well. She'll have seen all she can by now. No sense in letting her freeze."

Katya nodded. She pursed her lips and whistled, making an odd yet pleasant musical sound, then waited.

In a few seconds, a dark shadow, one of Katya's most valuable weapons and allies, plummeted out of the misty sky.

* * * *

Three years before Day Zero

Katya had found Fayne on a solitary trip through the woods near her village during one of her infrequent visits home. Life as an Oathtaker didn't provide much opportunity for family life, so Katya treasured the times she was able to sneak away for a few days to visit her parents and older brother.

Still, home, or not, there was no sense in wasting a day. There were always ways to stay sharp, even improve, if she looked for them.

She had crept out of the house while everyone else still slept and walked into the woods she loved so well, planning to spend a few hours hunting for medicinal herbs and roots she was running low on.

She had observed a promising hollow log across a clearing, and while rounding a massive scarlet hemp tree, she spotted a small bird lying on the ground, barely moving. She looked overhead and noticed a nest on one of the upper branches of the hemp.

Katya knelt and examined the bird. It was a female hunting falcon with gorgeous colouring, a skilled and very dangerous predator. This one was close to death and so weak that it could barely snap at Katya's hand when she stroked the bird's wing.

Katya dropped her pack and scaled the tree towards the nest. As she neared it, she climbed with caution, wary of dealing with an angry mother falcon's sharp beak and talons. Not seeing or hearing any signs of life, Katya drew her eyes even with the nest.

Empty. Nothing but a few pieces of eggshell. No baby birds, no food, no evidence of any recent use. It looked like the wee falcon had fallen from the nest and had been abandoned by her mother.

Katya swung back down the branches to the ground. She took off her cloak and wrapped the bird in it, cooing all the while. Whether it was from her gentle handling or part of her inborn elven connection with animals and nature, the small bird stopped shaking.

Bird and elf made their way home.

Katya spent the next two weeks bringing the small falcon back to life. The bird, who Katya named Fayne, first lived in a basket in her room. Being fed a steady diet of bugs, then grubs and finally chunks of stewing meat revitalised the falcon as if by magic, and she soon moved to a perch Katya built next to her bed.

In short order, Fayne had graduated to riding on Katya's shoulder as her constant companion. It took some time, but Katya grew used to the falcon launching herself into the air to snap up a mouse or rabbit that the bird had spotted with her outstanding eyesight. She had a local blacksmith create a small iron perch that was stitched into the left shoulder of her chestplate. It was easier for the bird to hang on to and it was far better for her armour than Fayne's sharp talons digging into the leather.

Katya also learned, much to her surprise, that she and Fayne were able to talk through a language that wasn't quite bird and wasn't quite elven, but some combination of both. Within a few weeks, they could carry on a conversation and, despite the growing love she felt for the little bird, Katya's warrior mind also recognised that she had found herself a valuable ally for the battlefield. It brought the elf immense pleasure to watch the feeble bird she had found grow and mature into a beautiful bird of prey.

She had no idea how much the bird returned that love and devotion until one night when a very large and very drunk human decided that he should try his luck at compelling Katya to be his company for the evening.

The drunk and several of his friends, sitting at the next table, had grown increasingly loud and obnoxious as the night went on, to the point that Katya and her brother Elias had ended up having to almost shout to be heard.

One of the men took a shining to Katya and began directing suggestive comments her way, punctuated each time by the boisterous laughs of his companions.

The siblings, who had been trying to enjoy a drink together without the presence of their parents — whom they both dearly loved, but needed to escape from on occasion — decided the best course of action was to leave. Elias dropped a few coins on the table and brother and sister headed for the exit.

The unlucky human, whose name Katya had never bothered to learn, stepped in front of them paces from the door, the first mistake he would be making in the span of a few seconds.

"Come on, love. I only need your company for an hour or so." He laughed at his own joke, as did the other men at the table he had staggered from.

Katya took a deep breath to slow the adrenaline that was already beginning to pump through her body. Regardless of the low-key circumstances, this was a conflict, and her body was getting ready to fight. She needed to stay calm.

"No, thank you. You're not my type. At all. Even if you were, I don't think you'd be much company anyways. Move." She reached for the door handle.

The humour on the man's face disappeared and his eyes narrowed. She had wounded his pride, and he grinned the grin of a tomcat thinking it was about to play with a cornered rat.

"I'm not asking nicely anymore." He reached out and, making his second mistake, attempted to grab the elf's arm.

As it happened, there were several ways Katya could have countered his clumsy grab. She was deciding between breaking his hand or spraining it when the matter was literally taken out of her hands.

With a screech that would later be compared in countless retellings to that of a demon, Fayne rocketed from Katya's shoulder and landed talons-first on the chest of her assailant, sinking her beak deep into the human's shoulder muscle. The man's screams joined those of the bird as Fayne drew blood and her wings beat at the sides of his head.

The man attempted to grab the bird and was rewarded with a deep bite to the back of his hand. He sank to the floor, protecting his face as much as possible.

"Please! Make it stop!" He could barely be heard over the angry screeching of the enraged bird.

Katya was shocked but called Fayne back to her shoulder. With obvious reluctance, Fayne released the man from her grip and flew to Katya, settling back to her shoulder. The elf could feel the bird's heart hammering away, making her realise how much it had taken out of Fayne to protect her. Still, the bird's eyes were fixed on the man she had just pummelled, cold and black as onyx, and Katya had no doubt she would attack again if provoked.

Despite the awkwardness of the situation, she half-smiled at what her new companion was capable of.

No one in the tavern spoke, most shocked into silence. Katya turned and looked at the crowd, seeing a combination of incredulity and fear on faces. One of the man's friends started to rise from his chair but sat down again at a sharp squawk from Fayne.

Elias put his hand on Katya's other shoulder. "Come on, Kat. Let's go." They left the tavern, and by the next morning, it was a well-known fact that to cross Katya was to cross her feathered companion as well. Many people in town owned hunting birds, but no one could ever recall such quick and fierce loyalty between falcon and elf.

They had been adventuring together ever since.

* * * *

Day Zero

Despite the speed with which the falcon descended, Fayne came to a stop over Katya's head before settling on the elf's shoulder in a rustle of frost-covered feathers with her usual grace. She was still small for a hunting falcon, but what she lacked in size, she made up in stealth, speed and intelligence.

Katya reached up and stroked Fayne's head, speaking to her through the trilling sounds they used. They went back and forth for over a minute as bird gave elf an account of what she had been able to see through the misty sky.

When the conversation was over, Katya removed a dried grub from a belt pouch and flicked it towards her shoulder. Quicker than the eye could see, Fayne darted her head out and plucked the morsel from the air, then munched away as she gripped the metal perch on Katya's armour.

War-face or not, amusement was apparent in Shira's eyes. "I never get tired of watching that."

"What?"

"You and that bird. Like you're of one mind."

Katya smiled. The old ranger wasn't far off. She considered Fayne almost as close as her brother.

Shira rubbed his chin. "What did she have to say?"

Katya continued to stroke Fayne's feathered head. "She can see a raiding party heading our way, in a skirmish line. They came from the larger encampment of them on the other side of the swamp."

Shira glanced into the swamp. "Do the raiders know we're here?"

"She thinks so, yes. They seem to be heading right towards us, slow and steady."

Shira sighed. "Not much chance of taking them by surprise, then. We don't have any elements of ambush on our side."

"That's fine by me. We haven't bloodied swords for weeks." *Not to mention seeing trade routes targeted hits a little too close to home for me.*

Shira's expression changed to frustration. "Katya. All these years under the Mark and you still haven't learned. Being a true warrior includes knowing when the fight isn't worth the fight."

She stayed silent, knowing he was right but not wanting to agree.

The ranger sighed. "Nothing to say? Fine, let me remind you. Remember the slavers in the catacombs? The copperfly nest? The tidal pool? Those could have all been quiet hit and runs. But you wanted to prove yourself and the next thing I knew, all hell had broken loose and you were right in the middle of it. You committed the rest of us to the fight. We've talked about this so many times."

He sighed again. "I suppose this is my fault as the teacher. It's a poor mentor who blames the student."

Despite her efforts to stay calm, Katya's anger rose at what she saw as unjustified criticism.

"Yes, we have talked about this before, Shira. You took me on with what you told me was raw talent for combat and tactics and strategy. You said you could teach me to be a strong member of the Council. You taught. I learned. Lately you've told me time and again that I'm too quick to reach for the sword. Which is it, old man?" Katya's heart raced, and her breathing came quick as she felt compelled to defend herself.

Shira replied, "You never stop learning, Katya. And more and more, I'm learning that I may have done you wrong in how and what I taught you."

The elf was stunned. "What? For two decades we've tromped around the world together putting evil in the ground. You helped me become whatever we needed when we needed it—a thief, a diplomat, even an assassin. Are you saying that's all been wrong?"

"Not all of it, no. But I've made some mistakes."

"What about the Council? Are they wrong too? We both swore the Oath—is that a mistake as well?"

The ranger looked frustrated. "No. Yes… Hell, I don't know. I've been feeling this way for some time. Reconsidering things. You and I—we need to talk, but this isn't the time. I need you to be cooled off and we need to be somewhere peaceful, not in the middle of a freezing swamp with lizard men bearing down on us."

Katya grew quiet again, breathing deeply to calm her heart and feelings. As she cooled down, guilt began washing over her. The old ranger was right. Her impetuousness had always been one of her weaknesses, and she gave herself to the joy of combat whenever she could. The three examples he gave her were just a handful among many.

And now that she gave it a bit of serious thought, it was clear that in recent months, Shira had been trying to reinforce virtues of restraint and patience along with her fighting skills.

To be fair, she hadn't given these teachings much thought because she was confident in the skills that had served well to keep her alive since she had taken her Oath. Although her impulsive streak had gotten her into trouble more than one time, Shira had always been there to set her straight.

But he wouldn't be there forever, and maybe it was time she began listening to him.

She shrugged the thoughts off. They would have to be reflections for later, not while a line of hostile enemies was winding its way towards them. She would meditate and start asking the many elven gods for the strength and patience to have a meaningful conversation with Shira.

Right now, she only needed strength.

The old ranger broke the silence. "Well, a course laid is a course to be followed. I'll speak with the others and we'll turn our minds and hearts to battle." The ranger turned and within a few steps disappeared into the icy fog.

Katya stared after him for a few moments, the guilt she felt still hovering around her like a second layer of mist. Next time they stopped to re-supply, she would buy cold ale and a private table so they could have that chat and she could apologise. Even after almost twenty years, she knew that if she allowed herself, there was still much she could learn from him.

Fayne's quiet squawk into her ear shook her from thoughts of ale and reminded her that she had a job to do. She oriented herself in the direction Fayne had told them the enemy would soon burst through the mist from. By this point, the clicks and whistles of the lizard men were much louder, leaving no doubt that their foes were closing in on them.

Keeping her eyes up, Katya began preparing her weapons, having long ago learned to find everything by touch. To drop her eyes even for a second, as Shira had drilled into her, was to invite a blade between the ribs or an arrow through the heart.

Katya had trained in many warrior's disciplines and could use almost anything she could lay her hands on as a weapon. Like all warriors, though, she did have a few pieces of her arsenal that were integral parts of her fighting style.

For attacks at a distance, she turned to a one-of-a-kind crossbow that she had dug out of a ruined temple a few years after she became an Oathtaker.

She and several other Council members had just finished clearing the temple of a group of cutthroat pirates who had been disrupting shipping and military routes up and down the northern coast. Collecting wealth and goods left behind after battles was standard practice. Anything that could be traced to an owner was — the Council had scribes whose full-time job was this task — but otherwise items were kept and used for the Council's never-ending mission.

Katya had opened a dull-looking wooden chest, not even locked. She was expecting perhaps some foodstuffs or medicine and was shocked to find a gleaming onyx and bone crossbow sitting at the bottom.

She immediately took possession of it. Although she itched to try it out, she needed to wait for a few anxious weeks while the scribes came to the conclusion that the weapon had no known owner.

It became Katya's, and even after all this time, it was still unlike anything she had ever seen, a beautiful combination of art and mechanical function that the scribes told her bore the name 'The Last Whisper.'

She sighed as she ran her hands over the familiar stock of the weapon. Given the thick mist and limited range she would have, the crossbow was all but useless here. *Not today, my beauty. Next time.*

When fighting in close quarters, she relied on a long sword with a square handguard and straight blade. Katya had also found this weapon, or perhaps it had found her, as it came with the unfortunate origin of having been thrust through her shoulder by a mercenary. The blade had been so smooth and sharp that Katya hadn't felt when it had pierced her armour and skin, and she only confirmed it had done so when she looked down to see the blade buried to the hilt in her body.

With a few deft manoeuvres, she had relieved the mercenary of his sword hand, then his heart, before removing the sword from her shoulder and wrapping it for travel.

There was an informal agreement among the Oathtakers when it came to weapons that had bloodied one of their number in combat — if they acquired it, they kept it. No scribes, no tracking of the owner. In all honesty, the scribes knew about this arrangement, but an occasional donation to the Scribes and Scholars Benevolent fund worked wonders at deflecting curiosity. Thus, Katya took immediate ownership of the strange sword, the likes of which she had never seen.

When it had come into her possession, Katya had begun to adapt her usual fighting style of using long curving blades. It had taken some time to re-train herself to wield the unusual yet magnificent weapon, but the effort was worth it. When she first used it, Katya had sworn the sword possessed a will of its own, that it moved quicker and cut cleaner when tearing into undead or dark-magic-created creatures.

A few hours — and a few thousand gold pieces — with a mage had confirmed her belief. The sword was indeed enchanted and had a grudge, for lack of a better word, against enemies spawned from chaos. While it was odd to have a weapon with sentience, it was another bonus of the remarkable blade, and one that Katya had learned to take advantage of in short order.

The mage also told her the sword bore a name, in a tongue that Katya never had been able to speak. No matter. The mage had told her that its name, 'Isshogai', roughly translated to 'For Life.'

It was an odd duality of weapons, as far as their names went. Black and white, when most things in Katya's life were generally grey.

Which she was fine with. She had grown comfortable over her one hundred and thirty-two years with being different, an enigma. No children, no mate, no traditional career, content travelling the world, poking through ruins and caves and battling the evil her brothers and sisters of the Mark hunted down.

Conformity was overrated, in her opinion.

Katya drew the longsword from its scabbard on her back, knowing from long experience that her fellow warriors were moving into position behind her. She glanced over her right shoulder, reassuring herself that Shira was there, his great two-bladed battle-axe resting on the ground. He nodded to her, eyes shadowed by his armoured helmet.

Katya whistled and Fayne lifted off from her perch. In battle, she would stay close by, attacking targets of opportunity and providing information through her outstanding vision and the connection to her elven companion. It sometimes proved difficult to focus on both close combat and Fayne's chatter, but she had long ago learned that her falcon's intelligence and perception made it well worth it to split her attention.

A staggered line of lizard men was now within sight, appearing like apparitions through the mist. As Fayne had told them, the brutes were shoulder to shoulder. That was good — close combat under these conditions would be much easier this way than if they had been standing in a line front to back.

The party of lizard men was exactly how a merchant who had survived one of their attacks described — small enough to move with speed and ambush caravans, but heavily armed enough to make short work of anything less than a group of extremely skilled fighters.

Lizard men were extremely territorial, and the larger group this ambush party came from had decided to settle almost in the middle of two major trading routes. When they did so, they made it clear that the trade convoys that had been traversing the area for hundreds of years were intrusions into what they now believed to be their lands.

Dispatching this party was to be a warning, a reminder as to how the larger group should conduct themselves and a suggestion that moving to a new locale would be in their best interests.

Katya shuffled her feet, securing stronger footing in the sand of one of the larger mounds poking above the waterline. It would be ideal if they could hold the small bit of dry land and wouldn't end up knee-deep in brackish water while also holding off a pack of vicious and bloodthirsty foes.

"Steady, all." Shira's strong voice broke the silence. "Wait for them to come to us."

Katya breathed in and out in a slow and deliberate rhythm. *Inhale for four heartbeats. Hold for four heartbeats. Exhale for four heartbeats. Hold for four heartbeats. Repeat.*

Square breathing. Although her companions didn't subscribe to it, despite Katya's offer to teach the technique to anyone who wanted to learn, she found it most helpful to prepare her body, mind and spirit for combat.

Through her methodical breaths, she grinned. She lived for this moment—heart racing, anticipation and fear and excitement mixing with the thrill of pitting her body and blade against another.

After closing the gap as far as they dared while still maintaining their line, the lizard men rushed through the short expanse of swampy ground left between the two groups of warriors with deep guttural yells. Katya noted, to her annoyance, that the creatures were far more at home in the swamp than her group, their large webbed feet propelling them through the muddy water.

"Now!" Shira yelled.

The lizard in front was taller and heavier than the others. He wore simple fur armour topped with the skull of some unfortunate creature on each shoulder. Symbols of strength, of command. The alpha.

Katya had found her target.

She rushed her quarry, swinging her sword in an upwards sweep, screaming her own battle cry, giving herself over to the joy she took from fighting a righteous fight.

* * * *

As always, Katya would later remember glimpses of what happened around her, images frozen in her mind's eye. Sometimes she captured them in black and white, sometimes in full, bloody colour. When lost in combat, Katya experienced things as though in slow motion, her elven reflexes and decades of experience combined to make it seem like she was moving at twice the speed of her foe.

Katya had learned that it was always worth going back to review the flashes that her subconscious had captured, sinking deeply into meditation to do so. While she always enjoyed reviewing successes, she also knew that to grow and learn, she had to reflect on her shortcomings as well. Her meditation allowed for both, seeing strengths and weaknesses in her fighting style and often letting her pick up new tricks of the battlefield from opponents.

When she later thought back to this encounter, many things would stand out.

Fayne launching herself into the air to observe from the skies.

Isshogai, on its first upward stroke, severing the right arm of the lizard man leader. The howl of anger and pain ending a few seconds later when Katya followed through, spinning around, extending her arm and letting her blade neatly separate the leader's head and body. The headless corpse staying upright for a split second, blood spraying, the grimacing head rolling away into the swamp.

The surprise of the lizard man's legs kicking…the arm she had lopped off pulling itself along the muddy ground, towards the head of its owner. The head, for its part, continuing to snarl at Katya.

Kicking the head into the swamp, careful to avoid the pointed teeth, before pivoting to the closest lizard man in range.

The next quarry, brandishing a large, spiked club, rushing at her from the left with the club held high overhead. Sidestepping to the right, creating time and distance. Seeing the lizard man smile, observing the club rise a little higher in anticipation of crushing the elf—relying on brute strength, for some reason ignoring the cunning elves were known for, betraying his intentions. Timing her last step to the right to let the massive club whistle through the air, thudding into the ground in an explosion of sand and water.

Watching the face of the lizard man with the spiked club, now off-balance and struggling to retrieve his weapon, change from anticipation to fear and confusion. Taking a long step forward, pulling the hilt of the sword into her chest with both hands before thrusting it straight into her opponent's heart.

The lizard man slowly turning its head, blinking twice at her then crumpling to the ground, sliding off Katya's blade and leaving a sheen of brownish blood. Unlike his counterpart, this one didn't move after falling. It appeared destroying the heart guaranteed a quick kill.

Raising both her hands over her head and letting loose a bloodthirsty scream of adrenaline and emotion before engaging a group of foes who, instead of the easy fight they envisioned, were now finding themselves faced with someone who clearly relished cutting them down.

Smiling as she waded into the group, sword flashing.

* * * *

Day Zero – An hour after the battle

All ten lizard men lay dead, surrounded by puddles of brown blood soaking into the sand or trickling into the water of the swamp. Aside from the group leader that Katya had decapitated, the rest were in various states of damage, limbs hewn off and chests cut open.

It appeared other members of her party had the same realisation when it came to individual parts staying alive, as many of the lizard man remains were cut or smashed into small, harmless pieces.

Battlegrounds were never pretty after combat.

Much of the mist had vanished, thanks to the weak sunlight now filtering down through the ceiling of vegetation high above them, taking some of the chill out of the air.

Katya counted three of their party with minor wounds. However, Redbelly, a stout dwarf who was always ready to recount a raucous tale of nights spent drinking, had lived up to his name. A stone axe had cut him deep across his midsection and only the chainmail coat he wore had kept it from being fatal. Shira had applied a strong salve to the wound that would both numb the pain and staunch the flow of blood until proper healing could occur.

The plan was to head to the nearest town that had healers, let Redbelly sleep through a trance of several days and grant the group a chance to restock, rest and seek out information. To make moving the big dwarf easier, they had rigged a sled that could be used to pull him out of the swampy area.

Katya was sitting on the driest spot she had been able to find, tending to both equipment and wounds while Fayne preened her feathers.

Gingerly, she lifted a leather square on her right shoulder, checking on the poultice of medicines there. She hadn't escaped untouched from her fight. The spiked club of one of the group she had tackled headlong had grazed her, leaving a ragged tear in her skin, even through her tough leather armour. At first, she had been worried that she might have been poisoned, but the dizziness and nausea that occurred with poison never manifested. Between the enchantments in her armour and the soothing herbs, she was quickly recovering.

Shira walked over to her, settling into a crouch. "They were an ugly bunch, weren't they?" he said, as he put his hands in the small of his back to stretch.

"Yes. A few more of them would have meant trouble." She replaced the sword in the holder on her back. "How do you want to deal with the encampment of them?"

Shira stroked his thick beard, a sure sign he was weighing the situation. "We don't. The plan was to take out a raiding party and send a message to the rest."

Katya tried her best to mask the irritation she felt, but, based on his response, she failed to do so.

Shira exhaled, exasperated. "Elf, we just discussed this. We gain nothing with a march across the swamp through freezing knee-deep water, followed by a fight with more of those scaled bastards in a fortified position. That's too much, even for us, especially with Redbelly being hurt. We know the camp is there and can come back another day if it becomes necessary. Fayne can scout the quickest way out of the swamp and to a town big enough to have a healer."

Shira went on.

"Fighting just to fight isn't needed here. We dealt with the scouting party, and we avoid the camp. You know as well as I that the rest of the lizards are already thinking the scouts are overdue. It won't be long before this swamp is swarming with the rest of...."

Before he could finish his sentence, Fayne cocked her head, then shot straight into the air.

"What the hells?"

Katya stood. "I don't know. She must have heard something." Katya pursed her lips and called out to the bird. In a few seconds, she had Fayne's warbled reply, piquing her curiosity.

"She's not making sense. She said there's one lizard running through the swamp. A small one, much smaller than the ones we fought. And it's screaming." Katya strained her own hearing and caught a high-pitched sound that was steadily growing louder.

"What's it doing?"

Katya spoke to Fayne, now flying in tight circles over her head, and paused while she got an answer.

"It's just running straight towards us." By this point, the screaming lizard man could be clearly heard by all the party members, who were beginning to prepare their weapons again.

Katya reached for her crossbow. This time, with the fog gone and her enhanced eyesight, it would be an easy matter to drop the screaming creature before it got close enough to do any damage. She cranked the string of the crossbow back and waited. Like the sword, this weapon was also enchanted, and the onyx and copper grip of the crossbow hummed with energy waiting to be released, ready to fire the small purple bolts of energy it generated. She extended the crossbow to arm's length in the general direction the screams were emanating from. "I've got it."

"Wait," Shira ordered, putting his hand out and lowering the crossbow. "Let it get a bit closer. Can Fayne pop up higher for a better look?"

Katya trilled out to the bird and received a reply as the falcon flew closer to the green ceiling above them.

"She says she can see it better now." By this point, the screaming was echoing throughout their small clearing. "The water is barely slowing it down."

She waited as Fayne gave her more. "It's wearing some kind of armoured vest." Fayne whistled in alarm. "No, not a vest. It's wrapped in some kind of creature. Huh. A spider...maybe a crab."

Shira stiffened beside her. "Shoot it. Now. A headshot."

The screaming lizard burst through a final line of vines and reeds, coming into view. It did indeed have some long-legged creature wrapped around it, its large one-eyed head bobbing up and down behind the lizard man's.

The creature riding the lizard man had a stinger stuck into the spine of its mount.

Katya had never seen anything like the bizarre sight approaching them. "Oh, we *have* to check this out." Katya lowered the crossbow from the headshot she had lined up and shot the right leg of the lizard man off at the knee in a blinding splash of purple light and foul water.

Despite the damage, the creature kept coming. The crab-like thing on the lizard's back lowered its own long legs on the right side, compensating for the leg Katya had taken. Despite herself, Katya was fascinated at the connection between the two.

"It looks like some kind of parasite. I can't wait to see this." She took aim again and put a bolt square into the lizard man's chest. It was a solid hit, tearing away skin and bone. A clean shot if she had ever seen one.

"Damn it, girl, I said a headshot! Quit wasting time and kill the damn thing!" Katya couldn't remember the last time she had heard that mix of anger and fear in her mentor's voice.

Anger welled up in her. She didn't appreciate being spoken to like a raw recruit. "Fine." She adjusted her aim and squeezed the trigger again.

Before the purple bolt even struck, Shira shouted in alarm once more. "No! Shoot the monster! Not the lizard! Damn it, Katya, shoot the parasite!"

The bolt struck where Katya aimed, hitting the lizard square in the forehead. To her horror, the lizard man still didn't stop, but the screaming did. The parasitic creature riding the lizard man kept pushing the now headless body forward in eerie silence, closing the distance that had given Katya the confidence to take her time before a killing shot.

"Everyone down!" The roar from Shira further surprised an already confused Katya.

"I don't understand, I got it right in the…"

She never finished her sentence.

As the parasite-controlled lizard man got within a few arm-lengths of them, Shira shoved her backwards off the small island they stood on. Startled, Katya slipped and fell into the swamp, and was submerged in the freezing water, the crossbow dropping next to her.

While under the brackish water, she heard a muted explosion, followed by muffled screams and gurgles. Her mounting confusion and the shock of the ice-cold water paralysed her for a few moments. She hated not being in control of a situation and right now she had no understanding of what was going on.

Her paralysis didn't last long. She got her bearings and scrabbled back up to the small island, grabbing her crossbow while shaking the water from her eyes.

What she saw when she emerged numbed her in a completely different way than the water had.

Fellow adventurers, men and women she had spent years with, lay scattered around the clearing, either dead or almost there. Some of the dying were screaming. There was a scent in the air, a scent that Katya knew from long experience was venomous, toxic.

Katya ran to the person nearest her and knelt beside the dying woman. "Amrada, what happened…"

She stopped mid-sentence. The girl's brown-eyed face was full of dozens of small thorns. Katya didn't have to look closely to tell that each glistened with poison. After a few raspy breaths, Amrada slumped in death.

Even having seen more than her fair share of dead comrades, Katya was shocked. Thirty seconds before, the pretty dark-haired fighter who had sometimes shared Katya's bed on nights they'd both sought warm companionship had been bandaging a cut. Now she was dead.

Something rustled behind her. She whirled around, drawing a dagger from her belt, ready to attack whatever else may have arrived. The sound was Fayne, who had landed on top of the sand pile Katya had tumbled off and was now squawking in alarm. Katya ran to the bird, doing her best to avoid looking at the bodies strewn around her.

As she crested the small hill, she took in the scene before her. Shira lay half in and half out of the water, his massive helmet next to him, his eyes closed. His thick armour was dented, the chest plate covered in blue slime and brown blood. The armour had resisted the toxic thorns, but not the explosion, whatever it might have been.

Blood was leaking from the joints in the armour.

She hurried to Shira's side. While his body was free of the needles, his unprotected face had not fared as well. The healing enchantments in his armour were keeping him alive by slowing the poison, but Katya knew his death was inevitable.

Katya looked around. None of her fellow party members had been completely covered by armour or robes, which meant all of them would have the needles in their skin. If the toxin was as potent as Katya believed, given its acrid smell, they were all going to die soon if they already hadn't.

She cradled the ranger's head in her lap. He opened his eyes to look up at her and despite his pain, smiled.

"Good. It worked. For once, I'm happy to see that you were off-balance." His words were hoarse, strained. "You lived."

"Yes. Thank you." Katya couldn't speak at more than a whisper.

Despite the surreal nature of what she was experiencing, despite her mounting emotions, she had to ask. "What...what was that?"

Shira coughed, blood misting from his lips when he did. The explosion must have done more damage internally than Katya had guessed earlier.

He closed his eyes and Katya thought he was gone.

The old ranger wasn't done yet, though. Without opening his eyes, he answered, "It was what I was praying it wasn't. It was a brain scarab. They're very rare and very hard to control. I had heard rumours long ago that the lizard men were breeding them. Obviously, they were true. Gods, they're wily bastards."

He paused, coughing again. Katya knew it wouldn't be long.

"They...take control of a creature and use it to get to whatever it's ordered to kill. The poor devil it was mounted to would have been in horrible pain. That's why..."

"...it was screaming," Katya finished for him.

"Yes." Shira's voice was growing fainter. His heartbeat, which Katya could feel through her fingers at his unarmoured neck, was slowing. "They're full of very volatile gas. When they're young, a pouch in their body is filled with different things — thorns, gemstones, even insects. Always poisoned and all moving faster than an arrow when they explode. Those lizards..."

He coughed again, with more blood.

"... really wanted us dead. Brain scarabs are very valuable and never wasted."

He looked into her eyes, a distraction Katya welcomed... The flow of blood from Shira's armour was increasing.

"Katya." His gloved hand found hers. "You were my finest student and you long ago surpassed me as a warrior."

He paused to take a breath, an act that clearly caused him immense pain. "But you were also like my daughter..."

He continued speaking until he could no longer draw breath.

Even when he lay still, Katya didn't let go of his hand for several minutes. Rage, white-hot, was building within her. Welling tears burned her eyes.

For the first time in her life as an Oathtaker she had no idea what to do.

For many minutes, she knelt in the cold of the swamp, watching the body of her mentor through the darkening skies until the chill became too much.

She stood and gestured to Fayne, who had been sitting all this time on the sandy island. The bird flew to her shoulder and cooed, her way of telling Katya she was concerned about her.

After a few minutes of weighing her options in silence, Katya came to a decision. *When all else fails, go back to basics. Rely on routine and training.* She began moving around the clearing, doing as she had been taught.

It was either that or die in the swamp like almost everyone else she cared about.

Chapter Two

Six months after Day Zero

"I don't even know why I'm here."

In response to Katya's blunt assertion, Athena Ebonywood smiled, leaned back in the plush chair she was sitting in and smoothed her long robe. "You're not the first. Eventually you'll begin to figure it out."

The two women stared at each other in silence. As Katya stiffened her shoulders, betraying her discomfort, Athena's relaxed seating showed that this was not a surprise to her, likely even expected.

"This is ridiculous. I've been roaming the world for decades, always doing what I needed to with a weapon close at hand. Now I'm supposed to sit here and talk my way out of a problem?"

It had been just over six months since the swamp. The thought of telling someone what happened that day...

"Correction," said the voice in her head. *"You mean what* really *happened."*

Yes. What really happened.

"It's not about getting out of a problem, Katya. More like getting through it. Consider it like the first steps of a journey to someplace you've never been before. I'm sure you of all people can understand that?"

"I prefer problem-solving at the point of a sword."

Athena smiled. "From what Jiris told me, that's what brought you here in the first place."

A scowl crossed Katya's face. "That damn greyling. I thought healers were supposed to keep secrets."

Greylings were among the finest scholars and healers to be found anywhere. They were intelligent and curious folk, shorter than humans, usually found hunting through thick books or hovering over someone or something that needed to be patched up.

They were also grumpy, impatient and honest in their appraisal of the qualities, both good and bad, of those they treated. In that sense, Jiris was an excellent example of the greyling race.

"We talked healer to healer. Outside anyone you might talk to about our chats, no one else will ever know."

"I see." Katya leaned back into her chair, trying to appear comfortable. It wasn't a state of being that she was used to. "What else did he tell you?"

"That you came to him terribly wounded after a horrific battle. That you needed time to heal, left for a short while against his advice and wouldn't give yourself any respite. You wake up at night soaked in sweat, having nightmares, which you deny. That you've tried finding solace at the bottom of mugs and bottles. Finally, you agreed to come see me." She paused for a moment, her face quizzical. "Is that about right?"

Katya's face was expressionless. "Yes."

"Excellent!" Athena clapped her hands together. "I'm glad I have the story straight. At least the parts you told, at any rate."

Katya narrowed her eyes. "What do you mean by that?"

She leaned forward, bringing her face closer to Katya. "Just what I said. You told Jiris the story you wanted to tell him, which is at least partly true. I know there's more behind those grey and gold eyes of yours. There always is."

Katya stared at her. "I don't understand this. All the talk. I thought you'd ask me a few questions and I'd leave here with some medicines and be on my way. I thought you were a witch." She glanced toward the robes and pointy hat hanging by the door. "A green witch."

Athena laughed at that, her short, dark hair bouncing along. "As opposed to my wicked black witch sisters. Or the sugary-sweet white witches. No, Katya, contrary to popular folklore, I'm not that simple." She once again sat back in her chair.

"Unlike most witches, Katya, I believe that potions and powders are only part of healing the body. Yes, yes, the remedies I can brew can close cuts, cure poisoning if given quick enough, even help regrow a limb."

She paused to take a sip of a drink she had beside her.

"But the mind? The mind is the key, a fascinating puzzle to be solved. I believe the mind must be examined and tended to just as closely as the body. I admit it's a somewhat...radical, shall we say, concept among my peers. I've been laughed out of more than one apothecary shop or library after trying to have serious discussions about these ideas."

Radical or not, Katya had talked to several warriors of all stripes in the past few weeks, and they all swore that the witch's combination of medicine and conversation had helped bring peace from the various plagues their minds endured.

So, despite her professed hesitation, Katya was curious. Curious, and desperate for some peace of her own.

Katya delayed speaking again, making a show of perusing the hundreds of books on the shelves surrounding them. Stashed among the books were jars and canisters filled with the tools of Athena's trade — herbs, flowers, dried insects, seeds and what appeared to be various pieces from who knew what creatures.

She finally said, "You say you're more than a simple witch. What's wrong with being simple? Sometimes simple is good."

Athena raised an eyebrow. "You may be a very able fighter, and I'm guessing much more than that, but you're not one for small talk. Fair enough." She gestured to a quill pen and parchment lying on the table next to her, both of which sprang to life. The quill hovered over the parchment scroll, ready to write.

"Why don't you start with what took you to Jiris?"

"Hold on. Why the parchment?"

"I take notes of what we talk about. I've found it most useful for refreshing my memory from time to time."

"I don't want..."

"Katya, I assure you, your secrets are safe. The minute we're done, they'll be tucked away in my safe. The safe is in a Bag of Infinite Depth that opens for me alone. When you leave today, that brass owl by the door will scan your aura. The notes I make about you can't leave this house without the owl sensing that your aura is here. Otherwise, they turn to ash. I take the duty of guarding secrets very seriously."

Katya sighed. She didn't have any real objections left to voice. As if encouraging her, Fayne squawked in a tone that told her to get on with it.

"Fine." Katya paused for a moment to collect her thoughts. "What ultimately brought me to town was an ugly fight with a pack of lizard men…"

* * * *

Katya had been talking for over an hour.

"And after I was able to get away from the scene of the battle, I started walking. I ended up in Fandalore."

Athena nodded her head. "A stroke of luck. Our quaint little town is renowned for having some of the best medicine folk in the province."

Katya pondered for a moment. "I don't believe in luck. Fate, maybe. I like to think Shira pointed me in the right direction. If Fayne and I had walked the other way, I found out a few days later, we would have ended up in Goldenleaf, which is a nice town if you're looking to see a parlour magician or gamble, but not so great if you need to find something meaningful."

Athena laughed. "You don't believe in a life of leisure?"

"No. If my parents had their way, though, that's what I'd have. They wanted me to be a merchant or a jurist, spending my days leaning over dusty books or buying spices. Travel half the year just to say I'd travelled, seeing lots of places but never doing anything of substance. They're good people, but I think they feel a bit lost as to what kind of life I chose for myself. My mother more than my father."

Athena didn't answer, watching the elf with shrewd eyes.

Katya stared back, again uncomfortable with the lack of structure to their conversation. Silence was for when she was sneaking up on a guard or scaling the wall of a crumbling fortress. So, she spoke to fill the quiet.

"I have a full life. I swore the Blood Oath to give my life meaning after feeling like I spent years learning with no ultimate direction." She pulled up the sleeve on her right arm to show Athena the tattoo she bore. "Here. Marked for life." She tugged her sleeve back down. "It's what I am."

Athena maintained the silence for a few more seconds before replying. "Interesting."

"What is?"

Athena leaned forward. "You said that your Oath is who you are."

"Yes. And?"

"Wouldn't it be more accurate to say that it's what you do?"

Katya was having trouble seeing where this was going. "I don't see a difference."

"You don't? It could be argued that one is defining your life's work, the other is defining your life. That's a substantial difference, don't you think?"

Katya didn't know what to say. Her work and her identity had been wrapped together for so long that she no longer knew where one began and the other ended.

Athena reclined again. "There's no right or wrong answer, Katya. My wish is simply to put ideas out there for you to ponder as we journey on."

Katya was confused. "We? You mean Fayne and I? We don't plan on going anywhere."

Athena put her hands together in front of her face, tapping her fingers together. "Nor should you. I speak of a metaphorical journey, one of healing. Fayne will certainly be part of that. But I'm hoping that you'll let me accompany you as well."

She paused for a moment. "If you'd like, Katya, I can indeed give you some medicine that will help you relax and give you the chance to heal your body. I've helped many warriors get through the cuts, slashes and poisonings of battle. You could take it, pay me, leave and never come back. Give me five minutes and that can be done."

"But I can offer you much more than that. My calling is healing, like your calling is war, a profession as old as Nakall. Soldiers who kill for the sake of killing, or for pleasure, don't have nightmares. They don't have compassion for those who die at their hand."

"But you aren't a simple and mindless killer. You have compassion, that much is obvious in your voice, your eyes, even your choice of feathered companion."

Fayne squawked at that point, pleased to have been mentioned.

"Thank you, Fayne. Now, as I was saying, I believe you are conflicted. For as much as you say you love the thrill of combat, I have no doubt you often think afterwards about what your battles result in. Death, sometimes to those who truly deserve it, sometimes to those who aren't evil, but misguided and powerful enough to harm others.

"Those kinds of conflict cause different wounds. They wound the soul, Katya, the spirit. No medicine will heal that, no plant can numb it, and no matter how much meditation you do, you can't make scars on your soul disappear."

Katya was, despite her hesitation, fascinated at how the witch phrased things that she had been thinking for so long.

"But spirits *can* heal with the help of another spirit. One who will listen to, and not judge, someone who needs to relieve themselves of the burdens of things they have both seen and done. Two spirits can carry weight that one never could alone.

"I'm willing to be that spirit for you, Katya, because I believe in healing the just, helping them understand what they have done and why they have felt the way they have and helping them be able to close their eyes without old ghosts and demons haunting them."

She took a moment to adjust her robes again, and leaned far forward, as if she were about to share some deep secret. "But make no mistake. If we start down this path together, I won't carry you or drag you. I expect you to put the same effort into our work that you would into raiding an old temple or whatever else Oathtakers do. If you're not willing to do that, I will completely understand, give you your medicine and wish you well."

She then sat back and waited for Katya to reply.

The elf stared back, not sure what to say. Her thoughts were in a tangle. She had been so alone for the past few months, and had not connected with anyone in a meaningful way. Now this stranger, this healer, was offering to take her hand and give her some direction.

Which was something Katya desperately needed.

She sighed. As much as she hated to admit it, she could no longer do this on her own. Jiris' suggestions hadn't helped. Trying to honour her dead friends hadn't helped. Trying to forget hadn't helped. It was time for true help, time to let another spirit begin to shoulder some weight.

The alternative was continuing to feel like she was drowning in her own life.

"Okay. We do this together."

Athena smiled. "Excellent." She glanced over at a large hourglass in time to see the sand empty from the top chamber. The hourglass then flipped over to reset itself.

"We've made a good start. You're out of the swamp." Athena let that comment hang in the air, wanting to be sure Katya grasped its dual meaning.

"The next time we talk, I want to hear more about your getting to town and your time with Jiris. He's a crafty old greyling, but I love him dearly." She stood and offered her hand to Katya.

Katya stood as well, wincing as she did. The puncture wounds in her leg and right shoulder had healed, but the gash in her side still hadn't fully mended six months later. Jiris told her that it was a deep wound, so deep it had torn into muscle. It would heal in time. That time couldn't come fast enough. The sooner the pain faded into a scar, the better. For now, it was a daily reminder of the slaughter she had taken part in.

Katya put her hand out to meet Athena's. To her surprise, instead of squeezing her hand, the witch gripped her arm just above her wrist. Katya tilted her head, widening her eyes in surprise. Automatically, Katya did the same to Athena, squeezing as she did.

"How do you know the warrior's grip?"

Athena laughed. "I told you. I'm no simple plant witch. You'll find I'm full of surprises." She gestured to the door. "I believe you can find your way out. Shall we say two weeks till our next chat? I hope you can find some productive ways to occupy yourself until then. Wouldn't want you living a life of leisure."

To her own surprise, Katya laughed out loud at Athena's joke, which, she had to admit, felt good to indulge in.

Athena looked at the falcon on Katya's shoulder. "Goodbye, Fayne. Take care of her."

Fayne replied with a happy squawk. Katya wasn't sure if she understood the witch's words or just grasped her tone.

With a swish of robes, Athena turned and disappeared through a heavy curtain that was hiding a door into a back room. Katya watched the curtain swing back and forth a few times until it hung motionless again.

"What a strange woman."

Fayne replied with a series of whistles.

"Yes. I like her too."

Katya smiled a large genuine smile, one that touched her eyes, something she had seldom experienced in the last few months.

"Or for the past few years," the voice in her head reminded her.

She turned and walked out of the cool, dim room into the bright whiteness of the town of Fandalore.

Chapter Three

Six months after Day Zero

Katya enjoyed the hustle and bustle of the streets after her time inside the small but comfortable room at Athena's. She still wasn't sure if it was a store, an office, a healer's or some weird combination of all three.

Ultimately, it didn't matter. It had turned out to be a very reasonable place to talk.

As she walked, Fayne clucked to herself from her perch. Hunting falcons were not unheard of in this part of the world, but one tame enough to be left unhooded and unrestrained was. Fandalore was a fair-sized town, not quite big enough to be a city but too big to be a village, and it hadn't taken long for word to get around about Katya and Fayne.

Most people they met on the street smiled and wished them a good day, or just nodded. A few of them went out of their way to cross the street. Katya assumed at first that these people had something to hide or were plotting against her. She had asked Jiris about it after her first few walks around town.

He had answered in his usual grumpy way. "They know you're a warrior. Probably a pretty good thief if you wanted to be. You're dangerous and they're intimidated by you. It's not every day someone like you rolls into town." He'd taken a draw at his pipe. "Also, Greenleaf Spice Traders is well-known across the continent. People put things together quickly when they want to."

Katya had frowned. "So, it's not a secret that I'm here?" She hadn't been worried about anyone tracking her here, as she was confident in her ability to take care of herself—and, for what it was worth, the guard contingent here seemed competent. When she had first taken her Oath, she had fretted about what her chosen path might mean for her family—would they be targets? A conversation with Shira had reassured her that her family was fine. The Council protected their own and it was well-known that to attack an Oathtaker's family would result in nothing except the attackers being hunted to the point that no hiding place would provide refuge.

He had snorted, which Katya knew by now was his way of laughing. "Elf, you were no secret by the evening you first limped through the town gates."

Katya hadn't quite known how to take that at the time, and she still didn't.

Of course, the night she had cut up at the tavern with the crooked gamblers likely had something to do with some of the people who wanted to cross the road and be out of her path...

She sighed. That had been a bad night that still lingered in her memory. Maybe these talks with Athena would help with that, too.

She stopped at a booth in the main market that sold meats, both common and exotic, and picked out a small sack of dried fish. Fayne rustled on her perch, knowing what was coming.

Just past the market was a public fountain. Every couple of days at this time, Katya had learned, a group of children were there on a break from their lessons. She heard their laughter and teasing even before she reached the square. Katya had timed her first meeting with Athena so she could cross paths with the children before she returned to her rented rooms.

One of the children spotted her. "Miss Katya!" That was all it took. Within seconds, she and Fayne were surrounded by a dozen children. Fayne let loose a string of high-pitched chirping, as she always did when she was excited.

"Good morning! Would you like to see Fayne do some tricks?"

She was answered with a chorus of "Yes, please!" It was almost a ritual by now.

"All right, then. You know what you have to do."

As a group, they sat on the edge of the fountain, waiting patiently.

"Fayne, come." She held out her arm, and Fayne flew from her perch to Katya's wrist. The spoken commands weren't necessary, but Katya felt they added to the show.

"Go."

With that, the falcon launched herself into the air. Every time, at least one of the children would comment on how fast she was.

Over the next few minutes, Katya put Fayne through a series of spins, rolls and other acrobatics. The children watching, even the ones who had seen this before, were entranced.

It was good for the bird, too. Six months of life off the road meant that Fayne wasn't getting her usual work tracking or scouting and Katya was happy to give her a chance to stretch her wings every few days.

Then Katya let out a long, low whistle. She could see out of the corner of her eye that some of the children were getting themselves ready for what they knew was coming.

Upon hearing Katya's whistle, Fayne folded back her wings, streamlined her body and dove into the deep water of the central fountain. She was a small bird, but her speed created a very large splash, enough to spray the assembled children.

Some shrieked. Some laughed.

After a few seconds, Fayne hopped up onto the edge of the fountain, water rolling off her feathers.

"Shake, Fayne."

The bird extended her wings and shook back and forth, causing some of the children to get splashed with water again, triggering more laughter.

"Fayne, back." Katya extended her arm and the falcon fluttered to her. Before she rested, however, she made a series of hops and spins back and forth, like she was dancing. The children watching giggled at this new addition to her show.

Huh. That was unexpected. Apparently, her companion was beginning to enjoy being the centre of attention.

As soon as she settled into place, the group of children pressed in once more. Katya took out the bag of dried fish and doled out pieces. When everyone had one, each took their turn holding their chunk of meat out to Fayne, who took it with a beak that could nip off fingers, before flipping it into the air and gulping it down as it fell towards her. Katya was grateful that Fayne was accommodating as well as intelligent.

After feeding her, the children took turns stroking the soft feathers of Fayne's head and neck, the bird cooing with happiness all the while. After each child had a turn, Katya tapped the perch on her armour and Fayne rustled back to her usual place.

"We have to go, children, and you need to get back to school."

She was met with another chorus of voices saying goodbye. She and Fayne walked out of the square towards the Loyal Dog, the finest inn the town had to offer.

"Show-off."

The bird squawked back, sounding indignant.

"Yes, I know. But the little dance?"

Fayne squawked again, less indignantly and with a tone of embarrassment.

Katya laughed. "It's fine. They loved it and you were the star of the show. But now you're full of fish and I didn't even have breakfast." She walked towards the left side of the inn, where there sat a small yet very good café.

She sat and ordered a simple meal — hearty soup of the day, local bread and a flagon of house ale. It was a crisp brew that had a slight taste of sour cherries, and Katya had developed a liking for it.

For a while, a few months back, she had developed a little too much of a liking.

"Oh, it wasn't that bad, was it? It's such an easy fix. There's no pain at the bottom of a mug. You can always find some ale. Mead. Spiced tea. Cider. Any amount, any time you want. It will always be there. Salvation is only a sip away."
The voice in her head taunted her, darkening what had been up until that point a good day.

Katya supposed that was the nature of grief and pain. It was always there under the surface.

She sighed. The voice was right, but she couldn't go back to living in a constant fog. It was a slippery slope between having a mug of ale when she was feeling frustrated with the world and drinking herself into a blind stupor every night.

The meal arrived and it was excellent, as usual. She left a few coins on the table for the server, a cheerful and attractive human girl.

Elves were always in tune with the personalities of others. No one survived as a warrior as she had without constantly being aware of their surroundings. More than once, Katya had caught the girl peeking around the corner of the kitchen wall as she ate, almost as if she were studying her.

After Katya had taken her first few meals at the café, she had been both amused and surprised when the girl had started wearing her hair in the same fashion as Katya. Katya had seen no other female in town styling her hair in the same way, and had they done so, she definitely would have noticed.

Like most elves, Katya had long hair, but unlike most, her hair was a striking red. Adding to the unusual colour was how she wore it—wrapped into one long braid and secured with a leather cord. Although Katya was not one for decoration, she did have a small collection of charms on the cord, mostly related to various elven gods.

For luck.

When the blonde girl had appeared one morning to take Katya's order for breakfast, the long hair that had been worn loose straight down her back the day before had been braided into one length and tied off with a short length of rope.

Although neither of them mentioned it, Katya had come to the inevitable, and embarrassing, conclusion that she was the girl's inspiration.

"Embarrassed? Let's be honest, girl, you're flattered. And intrigued," her inner voice had argued at the time.

That had been another one of those days that Katya could take or leave her internal conversations. It became exhausting going back and forth with herself.

"Fayne, for the first time in my life, I'm a trendsetter," she had said on the day Lili had changed her hair.

The falcon had replied with the bird equivalent of rolling eyes.

Being who she was, though, Katya also took the opportunity to watch and learn about the blonde girl, whose full name she came to learn was Lili Fallendew. Katya occasionally saw Lili in the town square or in the market, sitting with a group of friends at an outdoor tavern table or shopping.

Katya noticed she laughed constantly, and with sincerity, listening and responding to her companions. She wore stylish but simple clothing, carrying herself with confidence.

But Katya spotted other things as well. Lili's gaze often took in the whole of the square, tracking who wandered in and out. Although she emphasised points of conversation with her hands, she held them free and clear of anything, like she was keeping herself ready to use them for something more than illustrating what she had said. She carried her coin purse tied to her belt and was careful to shield her movements when opening or securing it.

While most people would think nothing of these minor details, Katya was impressed. They showed that Lili was a cautious and thoughtful girl who also maintained a fun and joyous lifestyle befitting a young adult.

A lifestyle that Katya, with a surprising pang of jealousy, knew she had never had herself, which sometimes made her wonder if her parents had been right about living a more traditional elvish life.

Still, the cheery girl had struck a chord in Katya, and she had come to look forward to Lili's daily greetings at mealtime.

"Hmm. Is that all you look forward to? She's very attractive. She's clearly taken with you."

She told the voice in her head to stop its foolishness,

After lunch, both elf and bird made their way into the coolness of the inn proper, stopping just inside the door for a few seconds to let Katya's eyes adjust. Although her enhanced eyesight adapted quicker to the dimness than most other races, and she felt reasonably safe in the inn, some precautions couldn't be ignored.

They made their way to the suite Katya had made home for the last few months – a large sitting room, a bathroom and a storage closet, all connected by a central circular bedroom. As an extra measure, Katya had purchased a lockset for the closet and added it herself. She would pay for the damage to the door and wall when she left the inn for good – it was a small price for being able to store the tools of her trade with confidence.

From down the hall, Katya spotted what looked like parchment attached to her door. As she drew nearer, she saw it was an envelope, with her name and the name of the inn and town on it, stuck to the door with a small pin. She plucked it off the door and turned it over. It was sealed with dark green wax bearing her bloodline crest, a stylised leaf that played on the family's last name.

She gave Fayne the letter to hold, and the bird gently took it in her beak, not wanting to tear the paper. With her left hand, Katya unlocked and opened the door. In her right hand was a new axinite dagger that she had bought to replace the one lost during Day Zero, as she had taken to calling it.

Precautions. They kept her alive.

Finding her room empty, Katya took off the weapons at her back and undid the belt holding the rest of her arsenal. She released the clasps holding her chest plate in place and hung it in the closet. It felt good to be able to wear just her bodysuit.

Well, a new bodysuit. To go with the new dagger. She had disposed of the suit she had been wearing on Day Zero months ago. Not long after arriving in Fandalore, while slipping the suit on one morning, she had been met with a wave of panic and sadness. She had meditated through the emotions, but that afternoon, she had purchased a new bodysuit and burned her old one.

After retrieving the letter from Fayne, now resting on her perch, Katya opened the envelope and began to read.

Dear Kat.

Her family were the only ones who could call her Kat.

Well, maybe she'd let Fayne get away with it.

It took a few months for your letter to get here. You know the courier system in this part of the world is pretty good, but all it takes is for a letter to get stuck in some backwater and it could sit for weeks.

Kat, I am so sorry for what happened. I know that sounds hollow, but I don't know what other words to use. I met Shira a handful of times, but he struck me as a noble, honourable man. Plus you trusted and respected him, and that was good enough for me.

When reading that, Katya had to fight back a lump in her throat. Her brother always knew how to put things in the kindest way possible. It was part of the reason he was such a successful trader — he was a gifted speaker, he treated his employees well, was firm but fair with them and made sure they had everything they needed to be their best.

As you requested, I didn't tell Mother and Father everything. I didn't think they needed a blow-by-blow account of Day Zero, as you called it. I go back and read the story again from time to time and I still can't believe it. I just told them that Shira and your friends perished during a massive battle and that he had died to make sure you lived.

Technically, that was correct. She didn't like keeping the details from her parents, but if they heard everything that had happened to her since she had taken her Oath, they would forever have no peace when it came to her life.

I told them that you had linked up with another group and that you were carrying on after you spent some time healing. It seemed easier.

I'm glad you found a safe spot to rest and recover, Kat. Fandalore sounds like it has everything you need. I've never been there as it's not on any of the trade routes that I run, but I hear good things about it. I hope you're still there by the time this letter finds you, or, if you've gone, that you left a way for them to get it to you.

I hope you are healing, Kat. Obviously, what happened took a lot out of your body, mind and spirit. I pray to the gods that you have left life on the road for a while, to start getting yourself back to the old Kat. I'm no warrior, but I know my little sister well enough to put myself in your shoes and can imagine what it would be like to have so much taken from you all at once.

At this point, Katya let the tears flow.

I don't know how you are fixed for money, but you can always use the company's credit house for anything you need. I hope you still have your letters of accounting and transit.

She did. They were tucked away in the innermost pocket of her armour. She had never had to use them to access family funds, as time spent searching through haunted tombs, deserted castles and collapsed temples had sustained her financially. Her family had no idea, but she had coins and precious metals, gemstones, even artwork, stashed away in various spots across the continent, allowing her to repair or replace equipment she needed, and live in relative comfort during the rare times she wasn't travelling to her next fight.

But it was nice to still be thought of as one of the family.

I wish I could do more for you, Kat. I hate being so far from you at times like this. But I understand – a life around our home was never going to suit you. I always knew you were meant to do great things, and you're doing them.

Here's what I can do – pray to the gods for your safety, send you my love and remind you that I will always be ready to listen with no judgement, even if it's only through a letter.

Mother and Father send their love too, and Mother wants me to remind you to wear a coat when you go out in the rain. She means well, Kat, but she still hasn't grasped what it is you do. Father understands, and I know he knows there's more to your last letter than what I told them, but he plays along for Mother's sake.

Take care of yourself, Kat. I am proud of you no matter what you do. I love you.

Elias

For a long time after reading, Katya sat on the edge of the bed, clutching the letter tightly while tears rolled down her cheeks. Without being called, Fayne flew to her shoulder and nuzzled into the side of her neck.

Katya closed her eyes and reached up to stroke the bird. "Thank you. You always know when I need you most."

The bird's reply was a quiet trilling. They sat together that way for a long time.

Chapter Four

Six and a half months after Day Zero

"So, I thought we could talk about how you made it to town and into the tender care of Jiris." Athena was wearing scarlet robes today, which on many people would be gaudy, but somehow, they suited her.

Katya had slept poorly. On top of that, when she went to open her shuttered window to let light and fresh air into the room, she realised she had failed to bolt the shutters when she'd retired for the night.

Her mood worsened when she stepped out of her suite and almost ran into the dwarven innkeeper, a cheery fellow typical of his race.

Katya hadn't checked outside her door, hadn't done any scans for threats or anything out of the ordinary. She was mad at herself, but transferred her anger to the innkeeper through a loud complaint that her rooms were not being cleaned often enough.

When Fayne attempted to calm the argument down, Katya snapped at her to be quiet. With a squawk of her own anger, the falcon left Katya's shoulder and flew off by herself.

At breakfast, Lili's usual cheery "Good morning!" was met with surly silence. Lili stood waiting for Katya to order, smiling.

Katya said, "My usual," and nothing else, before throwing the menu onto the table. It skidded across the surface and fell to the ground.

Lili was clearly surprised at how Katya was reacting. "Is everything all right tod…"

That was as far as Lili got before Katya fixed her with a cold stare, repeated "My usual," and turned away to glare at the street.

"Oh. Of course." She retrieved the menu from the ground, then brought Katya her food and drink a few minutes later. She placed it on the table without a word and left Katya in silence.

As she made the walk to her scheduled conversation with Athena, Katya kept telling herself that she didn't feel guilty about the obvious hurt she had caused Lili.

Fayne rejoined her at Athena's, still out of sorts, before they both went inside.

"You already know how I got to town."

"Hmm. A bit moody today. How are you sleeping of late?"

Katya paused before answering, debating whether she should answer honestly or not. "Horrible. I'm awake most of the night. When I can sleep, as soon as I drift off, I see too many…"

Katya stopped before she finished her thought.

Athena leaned forward, clearly wanting to hear more detail. "Too many what?"

"Nothing."

"Too many faces? Bodies? Too much death?"

Katya crossed her arms and looked away. "Yes." She stared back at the witch. "Are you happy now?"

"It's not about me being happy, Katya. This isn't a battle between us. As I've said, my job is to lay out things for you to ponder." She leaned back. "I can give you a wonderful sleeping powder before you leave. Stir it into hot tea at night and you'll sleep well."

Katya held her hand up, her index finger extended. "I don't want..."

"But not so deeply that you wouldn't hear someone presenting a threat."

Katya dropped her hand back to her lap. "Oh." She felt like she had to say something else, some small comment to show that she still wasn't happy because that was the kind of mood she was in.

"I don't like tea."

The witch sighed. "Katya, I know this is only the second time we've talked. You are clearly someone who guards her thoughts and emotions, and for understandable reasons. But if we are ever going to develop any kind of meaningful relationship, you'll have to learn to open those doors a little bit. I have your best interests at heart." She took a sip from a cup of light green liquid beside her.

She smiled. "Besides, dead warriors don't put gold into my strongbox."

Despite her mood, Katya grudgingly returned the smile. "Fair enough."

"Excellent. I'm glad we're building an understanding. I was hoping we could talk today about how you arrived here after leaving the swamp."

"Fine. After Fayne and I walked out of the swamp..."

* * * *

One day after Day Zero

After a half day's walk, Fayne's impeccable eyesight led them to a large, well-travelled roadway. The rushing stream Katya had been following ran under the road, covered by a well-maintained bridge. That was a positive sign—roads and public works in good repair meant that there was a fair-sized, respectable settlement nearby. In the distance, to the east, Katya spotted a cluster of what appeared to be buildings. This too was positive.

Katya was not at her best. Despite the healing moss she had put on her wounds, all three of them had started to ache again and were making the walk very taxing. She leaned on the bricks forming the edge of the bridge, lowering herself to a sitting position.

Katya sank into silence, breathing deep in an effort to stem the pain. After a few minutes, Fayne landed next to her in a flurry of feathers. She chirped.

"Yes, I saw it. A town is good right now. I need to get to a healer."

A short series of squawks ensued.

"This is a pretty big road. It has to lead somewhere large enough to have at least one healer. If we're lucky, an inn and the shops we need as well."

More squawks.

"No, I can make it. I'm hoping no one wanders along looking for a fight, though."

Fayne replied with alarmed chirps and whistles.

Katya smiled. "Yes, I know you're a tough little thing. But you're tired, too. We both need rest."

After some hesitation, Fayne spoke again. Her language this time was slower, more subdued.

Katya's face settled into stone. "I don't want to talk about it."

A few more warbles came from the falcon.

"I said no. What happened at that camp happened. That's the end of it." She stood, adjusting her armour to make herself slightly more comfortable. "Come, bird, let's walk."

Fayne tweeted with sadness, giving Katya a pang of guilt. She knew the little hunting bird loved her immensely and was worried about her, but right now, with wounds both physical and mental being so fresh, Katya had no desire to talk about what had happened at the lizard encampment.

Some time, maybe.

Another hour's walk brought them to the cluster of buildings she had seen, which turned out to be, according to an attractive sign on the main gate, the settlement of Fandalore. It was the size Katya was looking for — big enough to service travellers but not so large that it would be rampant with people and creatures hostile to an Oathtaker.

She hoped.

As the elf and bird had gotten closer to town, they began to encounter the occasional traveller, all of whom stared at them with considerable curiosity. The road they travelled was lined with clumps of homes that grew larger as they approached the town's outer wall, which was made of solid rock topped at intervals with watch towers. A guard post was built into the wall next to the gate, straddling the road.

Katya and Fayne approached the guard post. By now, Katya was in considerable pain. She had grown feverish, and the wound in her side was itchy and hot and had started bleeding again. There was a very good chance it was infected after all. As they drew closer to the gate, the guards on either side of the road exchanged wary looks.

Katya drew even with the guards, who were appraising her appearance, her injuries and the bird perched on her shoulder. One guard, his shoulder epaulettes marking him as squad captain, stepped towards her, suspicion obvious on his face.

"Hello, traveller. What brings you to Fandalore?"

Katya, with some difficulty, stood up straight. "I need a healer and supplies." She was finding it hard to catch her breath.

The captain craned his neck to look at Katya's wounded side. "So I see. Your armour is soaked through with blood."

Katya wasn't surprised to hear that. She nodded.

"Who wounded you?"

"A lizard man with a very large axe." Despite her condition, Katya was growing angry with the inane questions.

The four guards laughed at her answer.

"Really? Are you sure it wasn't some drunken farm boy or his jealous girl...?" The captain stopped and the colour drained from his face. While he had been talking, Katya had tugged off her right glove and pushed up the sleeve to show her wrist marking.

"Gods. You're an Oathtaker." He wheeled to one of his subordinates. "Go fetch Jiris. With haste." He pointed at another. "You. Help me take her into the guardhouse."

The captain moved to Katya's injured side. He gently draped her arm over his shoulders and took up the weight of her body. She sighed in relief. The other guard did the same on her left side. Fayne rustled, a bit agitated at the guard being so close to her, but stayed put on her perch. They moved towards the guardhouse as one.

"Begging your pardon, ma'am. We meant no disrespect. It's been many years since anyone who has sworn the Oath has come…"

"It's fine." At this point, Katya was gasping as she spoke. "Get me a chair and a healer and we're even."

The cool dimness of the guardhouse was a relief. The guards manoeuvred Katya to a chair and helped her sit. She pushed her right forearm against the wound in her side, trying to staunch the blood that was dripping onto the floor.

"Water?" she whispered.

The remaining guard moved to the next room and could be heard drawing water from a basin. He brought Katya a large tumbler full of cold spring water, which she drank in one go. She held out the glass and he scurried away to refill it.

Katya began to sway back and forth in the chair. The blood loss, the morning's walk, the hot sun…it was all beginning to take its toll. She closed her eyes and did her best to remain upright.

Fayne had taken up a spot on an overhead beam

Within a few minutes, in which the guards mercifully stayed quiet and didn't try to engage her in conversation, a rear door opened. Footsteps approached and stopped in front of her. She opened her eyes.

She was at eye level with a weathered greyling, almost bald, with tufts of white hair behind his ears. Like most of his kind, his body was covered in short fur, save for his leathery hands and feet. He wore a long black coat full of pockets and had a cloth satchel slung over one shoulder. A pair of spectacles perched on the end of his nose, attached to the lapel of his coat with a silver chain. He puffed away at a large pipe carved from blue stone. Behind his stern expression, he had gentle and curious eyes that matched the shade of his pipe.

"You must be the healer."

He removed his pipe and pointed at her with the stem. "You must be the patient." He turned and looked up at the guard captain. "Take off her armour. And be careful about it." The captain turned to comply. "Oh, and don't touch her blood. If she's poisoned in any way, it could be harmful."

Fayne squawked in apparent disapproval. The healer looked at the bird.

"Hush, or I'll have you turned into a duster."

Fayne chirped in alarm.

"He doesn't mean it, love," Katya said. She turned to the healer. "I'm sorry. She's very protective. There's no poison I know of. Maybe infection though."

The greyling harrumphed. "Fine, as long as it stays out of my way." He turned to the captain of the guard. "What? Aren't you done yet?"

The captain looked annoyed. "Hold your tongue, Jiris." He undid the last buckle on Katya's armoured chest plate and gingerly lifted it off her. As he did so, the extent of the blood loss under the jagged tear in the leather armour became evident.

Jiris' eyes widened in alarm.

"Girl, I'm going to have them take off your leg armour as well. I can see another spot where you're wounded."

Between the four guards, they were able to remove the knee-high leather boots and leather leggings that Katya wore with a minimum of discomfort. Under other circumstances, she would be irate at being stripped of her armour and weapons, but she needed relief and knew it was necessary.

He faced the four guards. "All of you, out. Close the doors behind you." Muttering to themselves about the old healer, they trooped out. When they were gone, he turned towards Katya and opened his satchel. He pulled out a small white cloth that a flick of his wrist expanded into a full-size sheet, which he lay on the floor.

"I know it's going to hurt, but I need you to lie on the floor."

Katya, who by this time was grateful for the opportunity, lowered herself out of the chair. "Gladly."

Jiris continued to rummage through his bag, removing instruments, jars of salve, more cloth and what looked to Katya like a jar full of fireflies. "You'll need to lie on your side. I have to get at the closure on your bodysuit."

Despite her deepening shock, Katya paused. "Pardon me?"

The greyling sighed. "I need to see your torso to treat the wound, as well as your leg."

"There's one on my shoulder as well."

"Of course there is. Come on, get at it, girl."

Katya understood. She rolled onto her unhurt side. With deft fingers, Jiris reached for the closure. When he started to tug it down, Katya stiffened. She knew the intent, she understood the situation, but she still couldn't suppress the impulse to protect herself somehow.

She heard another sigh behind her. "My dear elf, I've seen thousands of naked creatures of all types during my years doing this, just about anything on two legs and some on four. Some, like you, have been fit and attractive. Most have been average. Some have been repulsive. But they all needed healing, and neither of us want you bleeding to death over your modesty. If you were capable of doing so, I would have you do this yourself, but since you're not, you need to work with me."

Katya forced herself to release the tension in her muscles. "Go ahead."

The greyling tugged at the closure again and this time Katya didn't react.

"Thank you. Besides," he said as he moved the bodysuit down her torso, "I would think in doing what you do that this isn't the first time you've been poked and prodded. I saw your wrist branding."

Katya could only mumble.

"I'll take that as a yes." Despite his brusque manner, the old healer was indeed deft as he removed the suit, being as careful as possible to not cause Katya any more discomfort.

Katya inhaled sharply as the fabric slid over the large wound in her side.

Despite the severity of her wounds and the punctured chest piece, her bodysuit showed no outward signs of damage. It was made of a very tough material created from spider silk. Aside from adding a layer of protection from slicing and crushing weapons, it also resisted cold, heat and toxins. The nature of the material was such that any cuts or punctures to the fabric would seal themselves up, so the suit looked none the worse for wear despite the injuries to her shoulder and side.

"My goodness. That is nasty. An axe of some type, I'll guess. It's not a clean cut." He was doing a very good job of covering it, but the shakiness in his voice at the extent of the injury as he began sorting through the items on the floor was evident.

"I'm going to let these leechbees out. You'll feel them crawling on the wounds, but it won't hurt. They're attracted to blood, love the stuff. It's part of their process in creating a very good nectar. They also have the wonderful property of releasing a painkiller and cleansing agent as they collect it."

Katya heard the *pop* of a lid opening, then a quiet humming noise. A few seconds later, she could feel a brushing sensation on the wounds on her side, leg and shoulder, then after that she felt nothing there at all.

She was able to mutter "Thank you" before she passed out.

* * * *

Six and a half months after Day Zero

"I woke up the next day in the clinic between clean white sheets with Fayne perched over me."

Katya had relayed her story to Athena exactly how it had happened, apart from anything to do with what had happened at the camp. As far as everyone but Katya and Fayne knew, she had been injured during the battle in the swamp that had killed the rest of her party. She still wasn't ready to tell the whole story.

Athena took another sip of her beverage. "Where you were no doubt then treated to the old blighter's bedside manner?"

Katya smiled. "Yes. As soon as I woke up, he accused me of ruining his best sheets by bleeding through them. Then he grumbled around the bed cursing adventurers and swords and elves in general while he changed my bandages."

"Yes, that sounds about right. Don't let him fool you. Jiris is a wonderful healer. I've seen him do everything from delivering a centaur's premature foal to removing the arrow from the heart of one of the fool guards who managed to shoot himself in the chest during training."

"I believe that. His eyes give him away."

Athena paused for a moment before replying. "Yes, they tend to do that." She paused for a moment. "What do your eyes say, Katya?"

Katya looked perplexed. "What do you mean?"

"I believe you've already answered your own question. You said the eyes give things away. If you had to describe what your eyes reveal about you, what do you think they would say?"

"I'm not…sure. I've never really thought about it."

"Indulge me. I'll wait."

The two women, witch and elf, sat staring at one another for several minutes. Katya sighed and closed her eyes.

"I think my eyes look tired. Like I haven't slept in weeks."

"That's true. But go beyond that. You're an intelligent elf. I'm looking for insight."

Katya furrowed her brow. "Pain, I suppose. Loss. Grief."

"Also true. You said loss — loss of what?"

"Friends. My mentor. "

"Would you guess anything else? Remember, loss goes beyond the physical."

Tears welled behind Katya's closed eyes. She hated tears. *Damn this witch and her questions.*

"Loss of what else, Katya?" Athena continued to prod.

"Of myself!" She practically shouted this as she opened her eyes. "Of what makes me what I am. My training, my skills. My confidence. If I lose all that, I'm nothing."

Fayne rustled her feathers in worry.

"It's all right, Fayne. She's fine." Athena moved her gaze back to Katya. "Why do you worry that you're losing these things?"

"It's already happening." Katya's voice was shaky.

"How do you know?"

"Because I'm making mistakes. Making poor choices. My mood today? It's from forgetting basic things that have kept me alive for years. I could almost forgive myself for that, because it's been months and I haven't really had to be on my guard. But even a few days after what happened in the swamp, I was shaken so much that it almost got me killed."

Athena looked at her in silence. The intent was clearly for Katya to continue. After a long moment, she did.

"I suppose you're going to tell me that's all meaningful?"

The witch waited a few seconds before answering. "The impact of an incident like you experienced, with so many thoughts swirling through your mind, is very relative. It doesn't particularly matter what I find meaningful. The important thing is how you see it."

Katya slumped in her chair. "At first I thought just my body was broken, and that once the cuts and fatigue were gone, I'd be back to normal."

She took a deep breath before continuing. "And because I thought I was normal, I pushed myself into a fight. I could have died...should have died because my head wasn't in it. I haven't tried swinging a sword since. I don't even know if I can anymore. If I can't, what do I have left?"

She paused again. "I'm scared that it's not just my body that was damaged that day, but my mind as well." Katya's heart was hammering in her chest, and she focused on slowing her breathing down to calm herself.

Athena let the silence hang in the air for a few moments.

"I'd say that's a considerable bit of soul-searching you've done. For what it's worth, I believe your thoughts and your spirit were damaged from what you were seeing and doing long before Shira and your friends died. It's almost inevitable in your chosen livelihood."

Katya sat considering that before glancing at the large hourglass, which had emptied and reset itself some time ago.

"Well, I'd tell you the story of what happened, but we appear to be out of time."

Athena waved her hand and re-started the hourglass. "I have time. You have time. And coin, or whatever else you'll be paying me in. I'm sure of it." She gestured with her other hand and her glass refilled.

"Besides, I find you fascinating. I've never had these kinds of talks with another female, nor an elf. To be honest, I've never spoken with anyone who has been through quite the same ups and downs of emotion and thought as you have."

Katya let out a sharp laugh. "I'm the worst-case scenario?"

"In a manner of speaking, yes. That's not why I am enjoying our chats, however. As I hoped you would, despite your immense love for combat, you have a level of intelligence and compassion underlying your skills as a warrior that most don't have. At least when you let it show."

Katya laughed again. "So I'm an interesting specimen, am I? I guess I find that flattering."

"I'm glad. Now, please, go on."

Katya sighed so deep that it reached all the way to her core. "All right. It was only about a week or so after I woke up in those white sheets…"

* * * *

One week after Day Zero

"You damn fool elf. Are you mad? Are you sure you didn't get hit in the head and not tell me?" Jiris stomped on the floor with anger.

"You need at least a month to let the axe wound heal. It cut you practically to the bone. And now you plan on going back out into that swamp?" He paused to puff on his pipe, as upset as Katya had ever seen him.

"If you want to kill yourself, you may as well do it here, so I won't have to go out with the guards to pick up the pieces. I have some poison recipes that would finish you off slowly and painfully, just how it appears you'd like."

Katya continued to dress. She was moving, but slowly. Her side still ached, but the wound was closed, and the area was free of infection. "I told you. I left friends out there, and I won't let their deaths go unmarked. They need to be laid to rest in the proper fashion."

Jiris was now pacing up and down her room, still puffing away at his pipe. "How much do you think is left to lay to rest? After a week, anything predators and insects haven't already taken isn't worth the risk."

"It's about honour."

"There's no honour in dying for nothing. Would your friends want this — for you to go back to the scene of a battle that almost killed you? I'm a healer of the body, but I know enough about war to say the best soldiers I've ever met knew when it was worth the fight, and when it was time to…"

"Walk away?" Katya stared at him as she interrupted. "Why would you say that?" Her tone was suddenly icy, Shira's last lessons echoing in her mind. Those echoes brought out a deep ache in her heart, one that she didn't know if she could keep to herself forever.

But for now, that was all she could do. There was no way she was ready to tell the whole tale of what had happened that day.

Not yet, girl.

The old healer seemed surprised at her sudden change of mood, but he pressed on. "Because I know it to be true. Do you know how many creatures I've declared dead because they wouldn't heed that piece of wisdom? Hundreds."

"You don't know what you're talking about. You weren't there that day, and I'll never be able to make you or anyone else understand what happened." She finished tying on her belt. "Part of this" — she pulled back her sleeve and held up her marked wrist— "is properly laying fallen comrades to rest. I took an Oath."

He stopped pacing and looked up at her. "As did I. To do everything I can to preserve life, all life, and to do no harm. I can't stop you from going, of course, but I will tell you that if you walk out that door before you take more time to heal, you'll regret it in both mind and spirit as well as body."

For a few heartbeats, the two locked gazes. Fayne, sensing the tension, twittered nervously.

Katya looked away first. "I understand. But I have to do this."

The old greyling sighed. "Damn fool girl. Fine, go ahead. But don't come here looking for sympathy when I have to patch you up again."

He turned to leave her room. He stopped in the doorway, his back to her. "Elf?"

Katya sighed. "Yes?"

"Be careful." With that, he was gone in a cloud of pipe smoke.

Katya stared at the doorway until a questioning cluck from Fayne brought her back.

"Yes, we're going."

Fayne tweeted and whistled.

"I know you think he's right. But do you like the thought of everyone lying there with nothing marking their passing?"

The bird's reply had a decidedly negative tone.

"Well, then we have to. The sooner we go, the sooner we can be back."

They left Jiris' clinic, the business district then the town itself, on the long flat road back to the swamp.

It was a much different walk back to the swamp. Both elf and bird were in better health, full of food and water and ready to defend themselves if needed. A walk that had taken over half a day a week ago took only a few hours now.

Fayne was scouting ahead and found a trail off the road that weaved under the green canopy of the swamp, running almost right to the small sandy islands where Katya's party had made their stand against the lizard men.

Katya stopped at the edge of the swamp, just before the spot where they would drop out of the sun into the dimmer light under the trees. Her inner voice was chattering away.

"Are you sure you're ready for this? Can you handle it? They died and you lived. That must eat at you." The voice seemed to be speaking up more and more, usually trying to convince her to re-think a course of action she had set her mind to.

"Shut up. I'm fine." She said this out loud.

"Then why are your hands shaking?"

She looked down to see that, indeed, her hands were trembling. The cold. It had to be the cold mist that seemed to start hanging in the air at the edge of the swamp.

"The cold? All right. You live how you have to." The voice went away.

From above, Fayne called out in a mix of curiosity and impatience.

"I'm fine," Katya answered. Anything with hearing less outstanding than Fayne's wouldn't have heard her speak. "Let's go."

It was a matter of an hour's walk to what was left of Katya's party. As Jiris had predicted, predators and scavengers had been busy. In some cases, the bodies had been picked clean, leaving piles of bones amongst various sets of armour and robes. Some had been dragged off the sand and into the water, leading to bodies that were both waterlogged and half eaten by the large predators that lurked under the surface.

Katya took a very methodical approach to organising the remains. She collected what she could of each of her friends, trying her best to not let emotion overcome her. She placed each of their remains in the shallow water around the small islands, on the muddy bottom.

To mark their resting places, Katya stuck a weapon into the mud at the head of the body, then hung something marking the identity of the deceased on the weapon—jewellery, a helmet, a clothing scrap, whatever she could find.

She also collected the various pouches and satchels full of valuables that her comrades had been carrying, transferring them all to the largest of the leather bags she could find. The standing arrangement when it came to the riches of dead Oathtakers was that the survivors of whatever calamity claimed the lives would take all valuables, keeping some in compensation for the loss of their comrades. The rest would go to any family members of the deceased, or, barring that, a charity in the name of the fallen. Like most matters of the Council, it was efficient and carried a minimum of emotional attachment.

When she was done, she spoke a quiet blessing to as many of the pantheon of gods her brothers and sisters in arms worshipped as she could remember.

She sat to rest for a few minutes, taking a long draw from her waterskin and sharing some dried meat with Fayne, who was perched on a branch, quietly watching her companion work.

Then, when Katya could delay it no longer, she turned her attention to Shira.

He lay where she remembered, half in and half out of the water. His plate armour had protected his body, leaving it almost untouched by scavengers. To Katya's surprise, his head was also intact — aside from the poisoned needles — which gave him the appearance of being asleep. Katya guessed it was the result of some lingering protective enchantment in his armour.

She felt as if she should do more for him than she had for the others, befitting the role he had in her life. After taking a few minutes to examine the clearing, she had her plan.

Shira was not a small man, and his steel armour added considerably to his weight. It took all her substantial elven strength to pull him from the water and lay him out on the largest of the sand islands where the battle had been fought.

She crossed his arms over his chest, noticing how stiff his body was, how there was a crackling noise as she did so. She knew enough about the stages of death to be aware that would be the state of his body, but she still had to stop, turn away and take a few minutes to calm the panic and sadness rising in her.

Fayne fluttered from the tree branch to her shoulder, cooing softly, helping to soothe her disturbed emotions.

"Thank you, love. I'm fine."

She warbled back.

"Yes, I know I keep saying I'm fine. It's because I am."

Fayne warbled again, punctuated with a few chirps.

"I don't know what other word to use. Great? Splendid? I'm fine. That's the best I can do."

Fayne replied with several squawks.

"I wasn't aware that you had become a healer. Have you been learning from Jiris when I'm not around?"

Several sarcastic twitters followed.

"Well, then, be quiet and watch my back."

Fayne turned away, chirping in a bird version of muttering under her breath.

Katya moved around the clearing, cutting reeds. She collected enough to build a simple shroud over Shira's body, which she finished by placing a large square of bright green moss over his face.

She retrieved his massive two-handed battle-axe and jammed the handle into the mud next to his head. Finally, she hung his slitted helmet from one of the blades, completing the makeshift grave. It wasn't what she had ever expected for the ranger, but under the circumstances, it would have to do.

When she stepped backwards in the ankle-deep water to examine the memorial she had created, she realised that she had started crying.

She turned to where Fayne had once again perched on a tree.

"Well, I guess we've done what we came to do. Let's sit for a few minutes before we head..."

Fayne's cry of alarm coincided with an explosion of water and mud behind Katya. As she spun around, reaching for the sword across her back, a hair-raising wail split the cold air.

Katya finished her pivot more slowly than usual due to the water around her legs. She settled into a two-handed grip on her sword, right foot back and perpendicular to her left leg. This opening position allowed for a multitude of attacks or defences, no matter what approached her.

She widened her eyes in shock when she saw it.

What she was facing was a creature out of legend, one that Shira had talked about but that she never thought she would see because of its rarity and the unusual circumstances that created them.

A swamp lich.

Liches were undead creatures, born of dark magic. No one knew what drove them or what attracted them to scenes of death and destruction. Liches had a human-like upper half, and their lower halves had the appearance of ragged, torn cloth. They floated, which made them extremely quick and dangerous opponents. Katya started racking her brain for everything she could remember about the undead monsters.

Tendrils of freezing mist streamed off its body, crystallising in the air around it. The swamp plants and slime that had stuck to the lich when it burst out of the water were already frozen to its skin. The lich's long arms ended in three razor-sharp claws and its piercing yellow eyes glowed even through the light of day. Katya could only imagine what they would look like approaching in the pitch black of night.

The lich was floating towards her, and it once again screamed into the cold air. Was there some bond it felt with deceased creatures that had broken when Katya buried her comrades? Was it a vicious monster in its own right? Did it recognise that this swamp had been the scene of immense death and sorrow?

It didn't matter. She was in for a fight.

She backed up, seeking more secure footing, and the ground she was on started to slope upwards. After a few more steps, she was out of the water, which would give her much more freedom of movement, and on top of one of the sand islands.

The lich kept floating towards her, wailing from what appeared to be a mouth. Katya stood her ground, maintaining her two-handed stance. From her quick scan, the body of the lich looked solid enough for a blade to damage it. If the creature was composed of mist or something similar, things were going to be much more interesting.

Without warning, the lich darted towards her. She spun out of its path as it did, completing a full circle and slashing at its body with the sword as it went past. Its wails increased in pitch and volume when she made contact.

Katya expected the lich to stop and face her or dart off in another direction to prepare for another attack. Much to her shock, it streamed towards the makeshift grave she had created for Shira, passed through the reeds covering his body and into several openings of his plate armour.

Katya was transfixed, knowing what was happening but clueless as to how to stop it.

For a few seconds, nothing. Then, with agonising slowness, Shira's right arm stirred, followed by his left. His legs twitched, moving into position to lift the body.

"No." Her voice was a horrified whisper. "That's impossible."

Shira's re-animated body stood, reeds and water sliding off the armour. His dark eyes had been replaced by sickly yellow ones. Cold mist trailed from Shira's nose and mouth, which the lich pulled into a hideous parody of a smile. Rivulets of water froze where they were touching the metal armour.

Shira's body reached for the battle-axe and plucked it out of the mud. To Katya's further shock, it also grasped his helmet, placing it on Shira's head, highlighting the yellow eyes even more through the narrow eye slit.

The lich-possessed Shira flipped the axe into the air and caught it by the handle. The lich held the weapon across his body in a fashion so familiar to Katya that she couldn't believe it wasn't really Shira brought back to life.

"I can't. I can't do this." Katya said it aloud. She knew she was being foolish. She should strike now, before the lich was ready to fight, but couldn't will her arms or legs to move. What the hell was happening to her?

The lich must have heard and understood her. It spoke through Shira, in a hideous combination of Shira's voice and lich's wail.

"Goooood." The sound was the creak of a wooden door being opened for the first time in centuries. "Gooood. Youuu wwwwill dieeee."

Katya began to shake. It felt like the muscles had been pulled from her legs, but she knew if she fell or collapsed to her knees, she was dead. She forced herself to keep standing and began, through her mental haze, to form a battle plan.

Fayne had also responded to this situation with alarm. She had taken flight, circling the clearing, rapidly squawking. Her panicky chirps were what drove Katya to move.

Katya closed the gap between herself and the Shira-lich without her usual grace. Fatigue, shock and her not fully-healed injuries were taking their toll. As she closed in on the armoured figure, she swung in a wild arc, aiming for the arm joints of the plated armour, where the metal was weaker. She was rewarded with a loud clang of metal on metal, with no apparent damage.

At the same time, the re-animated Shira swung the great axe up and over in a downward sweep. The lich didn't seem to have any of Shira's combat savvy but was simply relying on brute force. Katya rolled backwards, ending up once again in water up to her ankles. She cursed herself for not moving as quick as she should have. A few seconds slower and the blade would have cut her in two.

For the first time in many years, she experienced fear when facing an opponent.

The blade of the axe lodged in the sandy ground, and Katya took the chance to reach over her shoulder and remove the Last Whisper. She jammed the point of her sword into the ground, cocked the crossbow and fired.

As much as she wanted to shoot at the head, the helmet covered too much for an effective shot.

The chest plate, however...

The purple bolt struck the spot where the exploding brain scarab had already weakened the metal armour over the lich's chest a week ago. Hopefully, a week of being soaked with mist and swamp water had weakened it further.

Even through her combat focus, she was amazed at that fact. *Gods, has it only been a week?*

The plate mail resisted puncture, but the crossbow bolt did dent the armour further, the force of the shot staggering Shira's body backwards into deeper water.

"Stay down. Stay down!" Katya was once again crying—not just tears, but deep, heart-wrenching sobs.

To her anger and despair, the possessed corpse was getting up again. Now she did sink to her knees, feeling that there was no possible way her legs could any longer hold her up. She had no further plan, no further strength, to carry on.

Fayne had heard Katya's anguish, breaking her own small heart. She burst from her perch, flying in tight spirals high into the sky, before letting out a fearsome screech and diving at the thing that looked like her companion's mentor, but was not him.

Before she struck Shira's body, she flipped herself so that her talons struck first. The force of the impact knocked the Shira-lich further off-balance, so much so that it fell backwards with a clatter of metal and splash of fetid water.

In return, the lich let out its own blood-curdling screech at having been thwarted. Fayne, who had rebounded off the armour plate, rocketed back into the air. As she did, the possessed corpse lifted one arm out of the water and launched a thin stream of frost at the small falcon from its palm.

The frost caught Fayne's tail feathers, instantly coating them in ice. With this sudden change in weight, she lost control of her flight and spiralled downwards. As she fell, her keen eyesight picked out a spot for what she knew would be a very hard landing. She managed to hit a patch of moss floating on the surface of the water near one of the small islands, bounced once, then lay still.

After a few agonising seconds, Fayne stirred, got to her feet then let out a strangled squawk. The little bird was down but not out. Gathering her strength, the falcon shook the water from her feathers and screeched with defiance at the icy monster.

The lich began to laugh through Shira's body as it once again stood, using the battle-axe as a support, the helmet giving the laughter an echo that made it even worse.

Katya knew one of the ideal moments to attack an enemy was when it was gloating, as the lich was right now. But the elf could barely lift her crossbow. Only replaying the memory of Fayne plummeting to the ground forced her to action.

Katya raised the crossbow again, firing another shot into the armoured chest. This time, the bolt pierced the metal and tore into the dead flesh beneath. No blood came from the wound, and after a few seconds, she realised that the lich's entry into his body had frozen any remaining blood.

Despite the chaos of her situation, she spared a few seconds to wonder how that was possible...it was intriguing, but distracting.

For the second time in a week, in the same spot, rage overtook Katya. Adrenaline surged, keeping her primed to fight or flee.

Katya chose to fight.

She fired one more time, and after the purple glow of the bolt's impact faded, she could see light through the hole she had finally created.

Another pained wail escaped the lich. Its yellow eyes met Katya's grey-gold ones, both full of hate for each other.

Katya closed the distance, plucking her sword out of the sand while moving, and swung from her waist upwards in a slash called ground-to-sky. The tip of the blade caught the edge of the ruined armour and cut deep into the metal. Katya tried to return the sword to a guard position to prepare for another cut, only to find that the blade was stuck in the armour.

The sword Isshogai was now vibrating in her hand, recognising that it was close to an undead creature, and Katya could hear the rattle of metal on metal. The spirit of the blade was waking up.

Katya was still trying to free the blade when the lich backhanded her across the face with an armoured gauntlet.

The unexpected impact knocked Katya off-balance. She lost the grip on her sword but at least gained control of her tumble and rolled backwards. While lying on her back in the water, she thought the lingering pain on her face was from being struck. It took her a few seconds of probing to realise that the lich's touch had flash-frozen her skin.

Her anger grew even more.

The lich was attempting to free the sword from the metal of the chest plate, taking advantage of the gauntlet's protection by pulling on the blade while looking down at the hole Katya had created. Isshogai, for its part, was thrumming with energy, fighting the pull of the magic that kept the undead lich in existence.

Katya was now without her favoured close-quarters weapon, but certainly not helpless.

In a pouch on her belt, she carried an innocent-looking piece of wood about the length of her hand — petrified wood that had been cut from an ancient spoolwood tree. Katya had found the branch while wandering the forest one day and kept it, thinking, if nothing else, it would make an excellent walking staff.

After a bit of research, though, Katya realised that there was perhaps more potential to the length of wood than she first thought. Some time with first a mechanist, then a mage, had turned the petrified branch into an amazing tool that was so plain that most people never even knew it was a weapon.

Drawing the stick from the pouch, she moved around behind the still-distracted lich, where she would be out of its line of sight. As she narrowed the gap between them, she moved her thumb to the larger of two knots on the stick. That was the mechanist's work—a small knot, when pressed, expanded the stick into an arm-length baton. The larger knot extended the stick to its full length, a combat staff that was almost the same height as Katya.

With staff in hand, she crouched and moved to within grappling distance of Shira's body, reminding herself to be wary of both the lich's jets of ice and the fact that the freezing armour itself was now a formidable weapon.

The lich, still distracted by the seemingly alive and angry blade stuck through its possessed body, didn't see her until it was too late.

With her left hand, Katya stuck the staff through the hole in Shira's chest, then gripped the part protruding with her right hand. She took a long step to her right and whispered a prayer that her weight would be adequate, the soft sand would support her and the metal of Shira's armour would stay intact for one more stress on it. She knew she was playing long odds, but it was the only gambit she had left.

Katya dropped her full weight to the ground. As she fell, she placed the soles of her boots on the outside of the lich's armoured leg. When she felt solid ground under her back, she levered backwards with both her legs and the staff.

The momentum she created tossed Shira's body over her, the lich howling with anger. As it flew past, Katya shot her hand up and grabbed the grip of her sword as tight as she could. It wrenched her arm and hand, but she pulled the blade free. The sword left lingering golden light where it had been stuck.

At the same time, she depressed the knot on the staff once more, reducing it back to its original size and clearing the hole through Shira's possessed body. The armoured monster crashed into the water behind her.

She somersaulted backwards to her feet and turned to face the lich once more, noting that her unorthodox manoeuvre had caused several things to happen.

The force of the throw had sent the lich onto its back. The right leg from the knee down was stuck out almost straight from the body. Using the leg as a lever to throw the lich had snapped it at the knee. Tearing the sword blade out of the hole in the body had further cut through the armour plate, completely opening it. The force of her staff being directed against the side of the hole had destroyed what was left of Shira's chest cavity and buckled the armour outwards. Cold mist was escaping from the spots where Shira's flesh was exposed.

Most important, the heavy helmet that had been protecting the lich's head had come off the body and into the swamp, out of its reach.

The adrenaline rush that had taken Katya to this point was fading. The despair she had felt since watching the lich enter her mentor's armour threatened to overwhelm her. Her body ached and a dull pain throbbed behind her eyes. She had to finish this.

With a flutter of wings, the now-recovered Fayne landed on Katya's shoulder. The bird glared at the remains of the lich, which were struggling to move Shira's heavily damaged body.

"Hello, love. You gave me quite a fright there."

Fayne chirped a reply, then a question.

Katya sighed a weary sigh. "Yes, I think we have to."

The lich drew Shira's bearded face into a snarl, teeth bared, while attempting to stand. It couldn't due to the ruined leg and the damaged chest of Shira's body. After some effort, with a clanking of torn metal, it got to one knee, but could rise no further.

Katya had no idea if a lich could leave a body once it had taken it over, or if it was stuck in the body it had possessed. She couldn't risk the lich leaving, not when she had it hobbled.

She stopped a fair distance from the thing that had been her beloved mentor, not knowing how far it could spray its stream of frost but not wanting to test it. Memories flooded her. The days before she knew him—hiding behind a tree, watching him put other students through their paces. The joy she had felt the day he had gone to her parents and told them he wanted to take her on as a student. The night he led her through her Oath ceremony when she became part of the Council.

Twenty years of adventuring at his side, surviving through more scrapes than either of them could ever count.

Finally, their last conversation before he died, as he tried to cement for her the lesson she had never grasped—that warriors didn't always have to fight, and that leaving a fight didn't mean that she'd lost.

Her chest hitched. Yet again, not heeding that lesson had led to heartache. Jiris had tried to tell her the same thing this morning before she had returned to the swamp where she had already lost so much, stubborn to the end.

She reached once more for the Last Whisper, cocked it and aimed at the head of what used to be a man she respected more than anyone else. A man she would die for. Had killed for.

"I'm sorry."

She squeezed the trigger and a bolt lanced out. At this range, she couldn't miss. Shira's now headless body toppled forward.

The lich did indeed begin to try to rapidly exit the shell of Shira's corpse, streams of cold air now flowing back out through the same openings it had used to possess the body. Katya had one more idea and she hoped it would finish the battle.

She let out a deep, body-wracking sigh. Taking up Isshogai, the sword that attacked the undead with such eagerness, she moved to Shira's body. She lifted the sword high, point down, and rammed it into the upper part of the armoured back, through what was left of the escaping lich.

With one last echoing cry, the lich twisted and lurched as it dissipated into the air, leaving nothing but ice crystals to mark its final death throes.

Katya hung her head, fatigue finally catching up, and dropped to her knees before securing her weapons in their various holders. She moved next to her mentor, laid her forehead against the cold metal and wept.

She stayed there until almost dark, Fayne watching over her. Before true night descended, she gracefully fluttered to the ground and nudged Katya into getting up.

Katya, shocked at losing track of time, agreed with the falcon that it was time to leave the scene of so much death once and for all.

They walked back to Fandalore by moonlight. The guards at the gate, recognising that Katya was not in any frame of mind for talk, let her through without a word.

Elf and bird made their way to Jiris' clinic. Finding the building in darkness, she pounded on the door until she saw a lamp flare in a front window. The old greyling was cursing and grumbling before he even got to the door.

"Hold on, damn you. I'm coming." Katya was, at this point, holding on to the doorframe. The physical and emotional effort she had put herself through that day had taken their toll.

The door swung open. Jiris stood silhouetted in the doorway, pipe smoking even though he had just awoken, wearing bedclothes and a robe.

"This better be good, whoever you are. I've been asleep for hours…"

He stopped when he saw them.

Katya was slumped against the doorway, exhausted. She had a large bruise and a burn on her cheek, her eyes red and drawn. Fayne looked equally as worn.

"Oh, my." The greyling's expression softened as he spoke, his eyes rapidly taking in her condition. "Are you injured anywhere besides your face?"

Katya took two steps into the clinic and looked down at Jiris. "You…you were right." With that, she collapsed, unconscious.

Jiris pressed a button next to the door. A few rooms away, a bell was ringing, summoning apprentices to help.

While he waited, knowing Katya needed to be taken to a treatment room, he looked down at the prone elf. Fayne, who had jumped from Katya's shoulder when she fell forward and was now sitting on the back of a chair, chirped what appeared to be a question.

"Exhaustion, I would say. Body and mind. She needs a couple days of sleep, food and some muscle salve." He looked at the bird. "Probably about what you need."

She chirped again.

"Go rest, bird. We'll take care of her." The apprentice healers picked Katya up and carried her towards the treatment room she had been staying in.

Fayne flapped her way to the perch beside Katya's bed. She watched the three healers tend to her companion until she could no longer keep her eyes open and fell into a long night's sleep.

* * * *

Six and a half months after Day Zero

"I woke up the next day and had to listen to Jiris repeatedly tell me how foolish I was. Again."

Athena smiled. "I'm sure he loved that."

"Well, in between complaints, he let me tell the story of what happened. He caught himself sympathising a couple times but covered it by calling me a 'damn stubborn fool elf' or some variation."

"Hmm. He didn't suggest at that point that you should come see me?"

Katya paused for a moment, embarrassed. "Well...he did. I didn't listen. I still thought I could work things out on my own."

"Which you couldn't."

Katya sighed. "No. In fact, that's when I really started spiralling downwards."

Athena nodded. "I think I may have heard something about that. There was a tavern brawl or two, if I recall."

The elf blushed. "Only one. I'm not proud of it, but I'll admit it."

"Wine, mead or ale is the commonest way most people, not just warriors, cope with things that haunt their memories and sleep. It's cheap, it's everywhere and it's a very easy way to pretend you're someone you're not."

"Well, I did a lot of pretending for a few months. I wouldn't recommend it."

"Nor do I. I'm glad you came to that conclusion." Athena re-settled into her chair. "Katya, why do you think you hesitated a few times during your fight with Shira's...body? Ghost? I'm not sure what to call it. From what I've learned, combat comes almost as naturally to you as breathing."

That was a question Katya had been grappling with for much of the last six months. Every time she thought she had an answer she ended up second-guessing herself.

What she did know was that, until Athena knew about the slaughter that she had caused at the lizard men's encampment, the witch wouldn't be able to truly help her.

But Katya wasn't there yet. She was building trust with the witch...but not yet.

"It wasn't Shira. It had none of his memories, none of his soul or sense of humour or compassion."

"Fair enough. Let's call it a lich, then."

Katya furrowed her brow as she tried to put thoughts into words. "I think...I think it was a couple things. Having to fight Shira..."

"You just told me that in your mind, it wasn't Shira."

Katya looked irritated, but Athena was right. "Yes, fine."

She paused again to collect her thoughts and decided that she should say what had to be said about this piece of the puzzle. Not only for Athena, but for herself as well. Keeping chunks of the truth she felt comfortable talking about locked away hadn't served her well to this point.

"I told Jiris that I had to go back to honour my comrades. That was true. But I also needed to see if I could still cope. Would seeing my dead friends make me freeze? Would I break down? That's what I wanted to process, and if I ended up tangling with something in the middle of it all, fine. I was ready for a fight.

"But when the lich re-animated Shira's body, I was just...so...tired. Not physically—I mean, I was, no surprise. But this was different. I was tired of...the mission, I guess. I thought I could wade back into that world of death, as long as the cause was noble, even after only a few days."

"It was stupid. I wasn't tuned in to the battle. Which scares me, because when you fight that way, you make mistakes, and someone will probably die. You or someone you care about."

She sat without speaking for a few moments. "If I can't fight, then everything I spent the last twenty years doing becomes...meaningless. I don't see how being an Oathtaker but not taking up arms could possibly work together."

Katya leaned back and looked up at the ceiling. "I need to figure out what this all means for me before I can put myself back together."

Silence hung in the air. To her surprise, Katya didn't feel as uncomfortable as she had when she walked in. Unloading some of her burden was already making a difference.

Athena broke the silence. "I think that's enough for today. You'll find that you're drained when you leave here—recounting events like you have been doing can often be almost as fatiguing as when you lived them. You of all people should understand the amazing connection between body and brain."

Athena stood. "Goodbye, Katya. Shall we say two weeks again? And please don't forget your sleeping powder."

Katya looked confused. "Don't you have to make it up for…?" She stopped, as Athena pointed to a shelf by the door. There, already waiting, was a vial of blue powder bearing a card that said 'Katya' in elegant green script. She smiled a half-smile.

"How did you know?"

Athena laughed. "I told you—you should trust me." She extended her hand and Katya returned the farewell. She turned and walked through the back curtain in a swish of red robes, calling out to Katya as she did. "Be careful that you don't start dumping too much grog into yourself again. Elves can legendarily drink, but mixing it with that sleeping powder would render you more unconscious than I think you'd care to be."

Bird and elf stared at the curtain Athena had vanished through before Fayne twittered a question.

"Yes. Very odd."

Another set of chirps came from Fayne.

"Yes. Both times I've talked to her now, I feel better leaving than when we arrived. I guess that's progress."

They walked into the bright sun outside of the little shop.

Fayne squawked another question.

"No, she's right. You remember what happened when I tried to drown my sorrows. I can't do that again."

Fayne replied.

"You're right. It wasn't a very good time, was it?"

As they walked down the sunny main street of Fandalore, preparing to make some apologies, Katya reflected on the months Fayne had spoken about. It was a time she would sooner forget.

Chapter Five

Four months after Day Zero

"Another one."

The bartender paused. "Are you sure, Ms Katya? You've already had more than a whole bottle of..."

"I said another one. What part of that are you having trouble with?"

The tender sighed. He shouldn't be serving the elf any more of the potent wine she was asking for, but he also wasn't keen on risking the anger that she had become known for as of late. The cool but pleasant demeanour she'd demonstrated since arriving in town had turned into surly silence, which, coupled with her formidable physical skills, was replacing the respect most people held for her with fear.

After a few seconds of mental tug of war, he decided it was easier to explain to the bar's owner that he had served the elven warrior more than he should have, rather than risk Katya's wrath.

Aware of the many eyes on him, he reached for the empty goblet, refilled it from a large cask of dark red wine then placed the full glass back in front of Katya. He tried to keep his hand from shaking as much as possible.

No one in the tavern could blame him, and certainly no one wished themselves in the position he was in now.

Katya held the bartender's gaze for a few seconds before grabbing her drink and heading back to her table. The message she sent was clear to all.

Katya, despite the prodigious amount of alcohol she had consumed, easily wove her way through the crowded tavern to the table at the back. She slammed the goblet down onto the table and asked, "Whose turn to deal?"

The young men she was playing cards with exchanged amused glances. They were successful gamblers, travelling through Fandalore on their way to the casinos of Goldenleaf. Even after a few hours of card-playing with her, Katya could tell that they still hadn't clued in to the careful veneer of civility covering her true nature, seeing only an attractive elf who had money to spare. She assumed that, in their minds, she was a pleasant way to pass an evening while lining their pockets. Perhaps even a bed companion for the night, if fortune smiled on them.

It would very shortly be brought home to them just who and what Katya was.

One of the gamblers, dressed in a fine red suit, smiled. "It's my deal, pretty lady." Katya rolled her eyes as he began shuffling the cards. She had never bothered to learn their names, and simply called them by the name of their clothing — Red, Purple and Green.

The four were playing Blades and Golems. On the surface, it was a simple card game. When playing for money, however, many obscure rules and variations could be added that made the game more challenging and increased the stakes.

Each player received six cards per hand. The goal was to assemble the strongest hand at the table. In essence, they were using cards to create an army. A player gained soldiers based on the number on their cards. Soldiers could be reinforced by special entities on the other cards in the deck — Generals, Archers, Dragons, Spellcasters and assorted other creatures.

These gamblers, both wealthy and successful, had a custom deck they carried. Katya had twice refused their request to join them when they first started playing. What had changed her mind was overhearing one of the men say, "Lich overcomes General. My pot, gents."

At that, Katya had turned from where she sat alone at a table and asked, "Did you say lich?"

"Yes." Green, who had won that pot, smiled. "We had the lich added to the deck and made it one of the more powerful suits, despite how ridiculous it is. Our little contribution to the world of the game." He and his friends had laughed.

Somewhere far away, Katya had heard the voice of the gambler over wind whistling through her ears. A lich.

Katya's mood, which had already been dark, had dimmed a few more notches. While it had nothing to do with these cocky gamblers — after all, they had no way of knowing what she had been through with Shira's re-animated body — she hadn't cared. The memories she had been fighting so hard to drown came roaring back to her with the mention of the lich. At that point, she had made the decision to do some gambling. Under the circumstances, considering her mood and level of intoxication, she had known it wasn't a good idea, but to hell with it.

She had smiled her half-smile. If anyone had really looked, they would have noticed that the smile didn't touch her eyes, which were hard and cold. A predator's eyes. "You know what? Deal me in."

That had been three hours ago. In that time, Katya, with her substantial experience with cards and deep coin purse, had won over a hundred gold. As professionals, her three opponents showed very few signs of nervousness, but Katya could see them. A blink that went a few seconds long. A bead of sweat at the hairline. Unconscious pulling at the shirt cuffs. Small signs, but Katya had spent years noticing the smallest details in opponents, no matter the situation.

Red dealt as she sat down at the table. There was a substantial pile of coins in the middle of the table, with a few gemstones among them. It was by far the largest pot of the night, and despite their nervousness at Katya's temperament of late, a healthy crowd had gathered around the table to watch.

Katya studied her cards. A six, a three, a four, a nine, supported by a Spear Carrier and a General. The other players took turns betting based on the hands they held. Green bet extra to exchange a card. Katya did the same, swapping her Spear Carrier for a Rock Guard, a good switch.

She studied her fellow players. Red and Green looked composed. Purple, however, was decidedly uncomfortable. This was the gent who had been pulling at the cuffs of his shirt and continued to do so now.

When he next did so, Katya noticed something. Visible in Purple's sleeve was a flash of white that had the rounded corner of a playing card.

She was unsurprised.

They were professional gamblers, after all. Cheating was part of the lifestyle. She was shocked at how amateurish it came off, though. Even in her alcohol-soaked state, she had seen it. Granted, details kept her alive, but who knew how many innocent people had been taken in by these three. She half-smiled again.

Well, let's play this out.

The pile of fresh cards on the table grew smaller while the pot grew larger. When the last card was drawn, it was time to reveal hands.

Katya went first, laying out her final hand. "Nine, nine, three, four, General, Rock Guard."

The crowd murmured. She had played a very strong hand.

Red and Green showed their cards, making elaborate shows of laying them down and exclaiming over their poor luck. Neither could equal what she played, leaving Purple to redeem their luck.

Who Katya had been carefully watching while his compatriots caused their loud distractions.

Almost imperceptibly, he slid the card from his sleeve and into his hand. At the same time, he dropped a different card and laid his arm over it, hiding it from view before dragging it to the edge of the table and into his waistcoat in a well-practised move.

He was smooth, no doubt. Most other players would never have spotted the ruse.

It came time for Purple to show his cards. He placed them face up on the table, one by one, naming each card as he did so with a slight tremor in his voice.

"Six. Six. Eight. Archer. General." Katya's hand had him beat at this point and he would need a very powerful card to win.

He paused before laying down his last card. "Dragon King."

The crowd murmured again. His hand had beat Katya's. He and his partners sighed with relief and smiled broadly. Purple reached for the now very large pot in the centre of the table.

"Wait." Katya's voice rose above the din in the wake of the end of the game "Don't you want to count the card you tucked into your coat?"

Everything stopped. Accusations of cheating at cards often led to lethal results.

Purple's face flushed. "I don't know what you're talking about."

"I think you do. While your partners made a big show of losing, you swapped a card from your sleeve. The Dragon King, I think, because I didn't see it anywhere else during any other hands." She leaned forward, her leather armour creaking. "Now. Are you going to show that card or do I have to take it from you?"

His eyes darted to his partners. Out of the corner of her eye, Katya spotted both subtly shaking their heads no.

"There's no card there." The man's voice was shaky by this point.

"Mmmhmm. The hard way then." With remarkable quickness, Katya darted forward and reached into Purple's waistcoat. She took the card and pulled it back to her.

"Hey! What the hell do you think you're doing?"

"Exposing a cheat." Katya took a moment to study the card, then flicked it onto the table. The crowd gasped as a simple two landed face up.

Katya glanced at the other two gamblers at the table. Now that their carefully laid plans were unravelling, their smiles and manners were gone. Both were sliding their chairs backwards, clearing the way to draw their weapons. Daggers, no doubt, as anything else would be impractical in such close quarters. It appeared they didn't equate the speed with which Katya had retrieved their partner's illicit card with any kind of fighting skill.

The crowd, recognising that the game had taken a nasty turn, backed away from the table. The bartender turned to his young assistant.

"Go get the City Guard. Now. Tell them she's about to be in a fight with three crooked gamblers."

"You want them here before she gets hurt?"

The bartender shook his head. "I want them here to keep her from killing them." The assistant's eyes widened, and he ran out of the door towards the closest guard station.

At the table, Katya was calm. Angry, but calm. No one had brandished a weapon yet, and if any of them were foolish enough to do so, she'd deal with that as needed. She leaned towards the centre of the table to scoop up the small fortune sitting there.

As she did so, Red reached out and grabbed her wrist. "What do you think you're doing?"

Katya stopped and looked at the gambler's hand on her arm, then at him. "Collecting my winnings. I'll thank you for taking your hand off me."

Red grinned. "I don't think so. I'll tell you what's going to happen. You're going to sit and have another drink with us while we figure out how to get out of here and bluff the town guards when they show up." He looked around at the retreating crowd. "And no one here will have anything to say about it, or we'll be back tomorrow with several friends." To Katya, he added, "You'll be leaving with us, and you can take turns keeping us company."

Someone in the crowd groaned, speaking for everyone in attendance. It was easy to see what was going to happen next.

Fayne attempted to whistle a warning. Katya didn't know whether it was for her or the three men, but she was certain the bird felt as if she had to do something before the inevitable fists flew.

Without a word, Katya pulled the arm that was being held quickly back towards her body. At the same time, she turned her hand palm up and caught Red's hand. Placing her thumb on the back of his hand, she levered his wrist inwards so that the back of his hand was against the surface of the table.

"Ow! Damn you, what are you..." The question turned into a scream as Katya, who had retrieved a carving knife from a pile of dishes stacked on a nearby table, slammed the knife through the middle of the gambler's hand, pinning it to the table.

Finishing with Red, Katya leaned back in her chair and placed the soles of her boots against the edge of the table. She thrust her legs forward, jamming the opposite edge of the table into Green. He was in the process of drawing a short rapier from inside his coat when the table hit him in the stomach, causing him to tilt backwards in his chair. Red screamed again as the motion of the table dragged him out of his chair by his pinned hand.

In the meantime, Katya reached over her shoulders, grabbing the back of the chair she was sitting in. In one motion, she stood, bringing the chair with her, and threw it over her head at Green.

The chair flew across the table and caught Green square in the chest, knocking him backwards and out of the fight.

Katya checked on Red. He was whimpering, trying to figure out how to either remove the knife from his hand or his hand from the knife, and failing at both. He was no longer a concern.

Without warning, Katya was hit on the side of the head with an object, not a fist. Pain rocked her for a few seconds, and she had to hold on to the table for balance.

Purple had, judging by the ceramic handle he was holding, struck Katya with a large mug. She reached up to touch the right side of her face. There was wetness there, and when Katya pulled her hand away, a mix of ale and blood covered it.

Rage built inside her, fuelled by alcohol, adrenaline and the strong emotions of the night.

The gambler's eyes widened with surprise and fear.

"I'm sorry. I don't want to fight you..." He was cut off when Katya stepped forward and punched him in the throat. He began to cough and gag, doubling over. Katya put her hands together and brought them down on the back of the man's head. He crumpled to the ground, face down.

But she didn't let up.

She knelt, turning the man over, and struck him in the face with an open hand. He did his best to protect his head and face with his hands, but Katya caught both with one of hers and pulled them over his head, leaving him undefended.

"Please. Stop. Take all the money. Just…stop hitting me, please." Purple was pleading with her at this point.

On one level, Katya heard his words, and they hit home. What was she doing? Beating a defenceless man over a card game? What kind of Oathtaker did that make her?

She was ashamed of what she had become.

The voice in her head chose that moment to add its opinion. *"Doesn't it feel good to get some of that anger out, though? Some of that rage? Who knows how many people these scum have cheated out of money? They deserve it. "*

"Yes, they do. They all do." Katya's whisper obviously terrified Purple more than anything that had happened so far. He was struggling to form words but couldn't.

Katya pulled back her right hand, forming her fingers into the shape of a blade, her fingers stiff. She didn't need metal to kill. She stared at the soft spot in the man's throat, ready to drive her fingers in and kill him.

"Goodbye, cheat."

Before she could deliver the killing strike, there was a sharp pain in the side of her neck. She reached up and found a small dart there. Another dart struck the back of her hand as she tried to pull the first one out. Two more struck her in the side, poking through her armour. They must have been extremely sharp.

She stood and looked towards the door. Several members of the City Guard stood inside the doorway of the tavern, holding small crossbows.

The captain, recognising the precariousness of this situation, was hoping to talk Katya out of this rage, or, at the very least, stall her until the powerful sedative on the darts took hold.

"Katya! Enough! Sit down!"

Katya began to feel light-headed. "No. These men need to pay."

The captain slowly walked towards her, wary of how fast she was. "They will. They'll be taken away and they'll have a trial. Or the gambling circles in Goldenleaf will get them. Something. But not you."

Katya realised that the multiple darts in her skin had been coated with some type of toxin. The lightness in her head spread to her torso, and before long her legs and arms grew heavy. She had to grab the back of a chair to stay upright.

"You…you poisoned me?"

The captain shook his head. "No. You're just going to sleep for quite a while."

Katya closed her eyes and shook her head to appear under the influence of the sleep toxin. Instead, she was running through several different methods she knew to both slow and dissipate the toxin.

The captain, while not as experienced a warrior as Katya, was no fool. Sighing, he raised his hand into the air and made a motion pointing towards Katya. The strings of five crossbows twanged behind him and Katya winced as five more darts struck her at various points.

After a few seconds, she dropped to her knees.

The captain knelt, putting a hand on her arm and meeting her gaze. His face was a mixture of sadness and sympathy.

"I'm sorry, Katya. This was the only way to resolve this without lots of people getting hurt."

The sleep toxin, combined with the massive amount of alcohol in her system and the fading adrenaline in her body, was becoming too much to resist. She had to put her hands on the floor to keep from collapsing.

The captain continued. "We'll take care of them. By the time you wake up, they'll be long gone. We should probably be taking you to a holding cell, but I'm not sure it would keep you locked up. We're going to take you to Jiris."

He stood before continuing. "But this can't happen again, Katya. You're too dangerous. You have to pull yourself together. This" — here he gestured at the tavern, which had not emptied as usual when the guard had arrived — "is not the place for you to sort out what you've been through. When you wake up, and are more in your right mind, I have a few ideas for you."

Katya, with tears in her eyes, had time to whisper, "Thank you," before she finally passed out.

The captain checked to make sure she was asleep. When he was satisfied, he looked around at the assembled crowd, then at Red, Green and Purple, all of whom were in various states of injury and shock.

"Does anybody here wish to make a criminal complaint?" No one spoke.

"Excellent. I'm glad all is well." He nodded at his guard, who took the three wayward gamblers into custody. Two more picked up the unconscious Katya and carried her from the tavern.

The captain took a handful of gold from the pile on the table and dropped it onto the bar. "This should take care of any damage and her tab. Have your boy bundle up the rest and one of my men will accompany him to the inn. It can be locked up for her there."

He looked around once more before departing. "Good night, all."

As soon as he left, the buzz began, and before long, the tavern was packed with new patrons who wanted to hear what had happened.

It ended up being a very profitable night for the establishment.

* * * *

When Katya awoke the next morning, she discovered she was lying on a soft bed in Jiris' clinic. She was undressed save for her bodysuit. She opened her eyelids, wincing at the bright light streaming in through the window in the room.

Feathers ruffled above her. When she craned her neck, she could see Fayne sitting on her perch, watching.

"Good morning."

Fayne replied, terseness in her voice.

"Yes, I know. It's not really that good, is it?" She closed her eyes as the memories of the previous evening washed over her.

She sighed. "Oh, Fayne, what did I do?"

The bird squawked for over a minute.

Katya was chagrined. "Very concise, thank you."

The elf sat up. "Oh, my head. I haven't felt this bad after a night of drinking in years."

"It's not the wine, fool girl. You seem to have a ridiculously high tolerance for that." Jiris had appeared just inside the doorway of her room. "It was the sleep toxin. It was very potent." He paused. "I made it that way."

Katya straightened up, despite what it did to her head. "You what?"

Jiris sighed. "I'm the one who made the potion and gave it to the guard. I've been watching you, elf. You've quite changed these last few weeks. Always angry. Impatient. Closed off — even more than you were when you first arrived. I noticed you were quicker to reach for a mug of ale or a flagon of wine. I know elves have a legendary ability to drink, and I don't know if any elf has ever drunk themselves to death, but you're giving it a fair go."

He took a moment to light and stoke his pipe. "I knew sooner or later there would be some reason to use those darts. I suppose the guard could stop you even if you were drunk and not in a mood to cooperate, but not all of them would make it out alive, making you a murderer. Or the guards might have no choice but to kill you to stop whatever storm you found yourself in the middle of. The darts were the best alternative."

Katya stared down at the floor. "You're right. They were very effective." She drew her gaze up, looking into the eyes of the old healer. "I'm so ashamed. I completely lost control. I fought with no honour, even if they were cheating thieves. I almost killed that man. Over a card game." She fell silent.

The greyling took his time before answering, puffing away as he thought. "Katya, what you've done is not out of the ordinary for someone who is dealing with memories that have been violently stirred up. Looking at the bottom of a mug is not the way out of this for you. It creates a false sense of security, which is something you don't want."

He drew at his pipe. "There's a fellow healer in town I think you should go see."

"What can he do for me that you can't?"

"She. And quite a bit, I would think. I'd never tell her this, of course, but she is a talented and insightful witch who caters more to mending the mind than the body. She has a shop on the Emerald Walk. It's quite a place to see, full of plants and books and who knows what else. I've mentioned your name to her. Whenever you feel ready to talk, she'll be expecting you. Her name is on a note by your bed."

Katya picked up the note. "Thank you."

The old greyling snorted. "Don't thank me. I'm trying to save myself some work. If she can talk some sense into you, I can stop patching you up every few days." He disappeared in a cloud of fragrant smoke.

Despite her throbbing head, Katya smiled as she read the note. On a cream-coloured piece of paper, in elegant green ink, was written, 'Athena Ebonywood. Healer of mind and spirit. Nine Emerald Walk.'

She slid off the bed and retrieved her armour and weapons from a locked cabinet. She had spent so much time at Jiris' clinic since arriving in town that she had started thinking of the cabinet as hers. She tucked the slip of paper into one of the many pockets in her armour, then left the clinic to spend the day resting and collecting herself in her room at the inn.

It would be two months before Katya made her way to Emerald Walk and through Athena's door.

Chapter Six

Six and a half months after Day Zero

Katya and Fayne stopped at the market for fish as usual, to perform for the children. Although, to be honest, Katya had started to notice that it wasn't just children anymore. There were more than a few adults who seemed to always have business around the square at the same time the children had their break. After her violent outburst at the tavern, Katya had assumed that many adults would stop wanting to have anything to do with her. If anything, there were more people curious to see the elf who had taken on three crooked gamblers and handily won.

Fayne, of course, loved having a bigger audience to play to, and Katya couldn't begrudge the adults in town who viewed her bird as free entertainment.

After leaving the square, they stopped at the café to have lunch. Fayne hopped off Katya's shoulder and perched on the railing around the small outdoor patio where they usually ate.

Lili walked to Katya's table, laying down a menu and napkin without a word, expressionless. She turned and walked away.

"Lili?"

The server stopped, not turning to face Katya. "Yes?" After a few seconds, she added, "Ma'am."

Ouch. If that was a jab at the difference in their ages, it landed.

"May I speak with you for a moment?"

Lili turned around with obvious reluctance. "How can I help you?" Katya noticed that she had taken her long blonde hair out of its braid and was again wearing it down. That caused another pang of guilt that her casual arrogance and callousness this morning had created so much of an impact.

Katya pushed the other chair at the table out and motioned for Lili to sit. She did.

"Lili, I'm so sorry. I had neither right nor reason to be rude to you this morning."

The girl's expression softened a bit. She had dark blue eyes that sat over a small button nose. Her skin was paler than Katya's own tan skin and had the healthy glow of a small-town girl who didn't need makeup or decoration to look pretty.

"You were simply trying to make conversation on a day that I didn't feel very good about myself. My mood had nothing to do with you or what you said."

Lili thought for a moment before answering. "I think I understand." She smiled. Katya couldn't help but notice that Lili's smile encompassed her blue eyes, unlike her own, which seldom stretched beyond her mouth. "We all have bad days."

"I would guess I've had more than most."

"I believe that. You have quite a reputation."

Katya raised an eyebrow. "Do I now?"

Lili laughed. "You have to know that you do. Not much stays quiet in this town." The girl's face grew serious. "May I ask you something?"

"Of course."

"Are you a mercenary, an assassin or a thief?"

Katya sat up straighter. "Pardon me?"

"Which one are you?"

"None. I'm none of those." Katya was flustered. "Why would you think that?"

Lili looked away for a moment before answering. "A few of the guards who were there the day you came into town are friends. One said that you were hurt because you fought and killed a bunch of lizard men for a rich king and that he paid you a sack of gold. Another said that you robbed a pirate lord and were on the run."

Katya could only stare. After a few seconds, for the first time in many months, Katya burst out in laughter...honest, genuine laughter. The sound of it was so unexpected that Fayne, who had been dozing in the warm sun, woke up and looked around to see what had happened.

Lili, apparently recognising this laughter as a rare occurrence, sat and waited.

After a few seconds, Katya composed herself. "I'm sorry, Lili. But that struck me as very funny." She sat back in her chair. Katya had to remind herself that, even though they looked almost the same age, the human girl was far less worldly than she. "Lili, do you know what the Blood Oath is?"

"I've heard of it and I've heard it connected to your name. It's a warrior's vow, right?"

Katya nodded. "More or less. It's an Oath that binds you to a brotherhood in which every member has sworn to hunt down and destroy evil in all forms. I'm one of their number, an Oathtaker."

"Hmm. Destroying all evil seems like an unwinnable task. What does that bring you into conflict with?"

Katya thought back over her many, many battles since taking her Oath. "Dark magicians and the monsters they create. Tyrants and military leaders who abuse their power. Slavers. Demons." She paused for a moment, before saying, "Even card cheats."

Lili, like most everyone else in town, had obviously heard about Katya's ill-fated card game. She nodded her head before replying. "I see. That seems like a very noble calling." Her voice indicated she had more to say.

"But…?"

"Well, it seems very…subjective. One being's evil is another being's life they were born into."

Katya hadn't expected such a profound remark.

"I mean, I don't know what evil really is. I try to read a lot about the world outside of these walls. They know me very well at the town archive." She smiled. "I've read lots of things written by mages and scholars. Philosophy. Alchemy and science. History. Politics. I don't think I've ever met anyone or anything that was evil. Mean, yes. Stupid, yes. But actually evil? No."

She adjusted her apron before going on. "I'm sorry if I've offended you, Katya. I may be speaking out of turn. I'm a server in a small café in a town that's just big enough to be on a map. My life is fairly simple and I have no idea what it means to have a calling or a purpose." There was a note of sadness in her voice.

Katya thought about that for a moment, trying to put herself into Lili's boots. It had been so long since she had taken her Oath that she could scarce remember a time when she didn't feel like she knew what she was meant to be doing.

Until the swamp.

It wasn't lost on Katya that Lili seemed to be as jealous of the elf's life of adventuring as Katya sometimes was of the girl's ability to laugh, have fun and live day to day.

Katya laid her arm on the table so Lili could see her Oath Mark. "This is what shows others, and reminds me every day, of having taken the Oath. It was given to me the night I became part of the Council."

To her surprise, Lili reached out and stroked a finger along the red lines that had been branded onto her skin so long ago. The girl's touch was warm. "It's beautiful."

Katya's stomach did a somersault.

Then, as if realising the somewhat intimate nature of what she had done, Lili withdrew her hand and blushed. "I'm sorry. I don't know why I did that."

Katya couldn't help but notice that Fayne was watching closely.

She smiled. "It's all right, Lili. People have done much worse. I have quite a few scars to prove that."

"I imagine. Waging war as a profession must be an interesting way of life."

Katya half-smiled. "You would think. But I'm beginning to wonder if it's really what I'm going to do for the rest of my life."

That was also unexpected. Why was she opening up to this attractive and insightful girl?

After a few seconds of reflection, Katya admitted that she had answered her own question. The intrigue she had already been feeling was reinforced by Lili's thoughtful and intelligent manner.

Lili, who recognised that they had shared a moment of some significance, stood. She reached out to Fayne and stroked the soft feathers on her head. The falcon stretched out her wings and cooed with delight.

"She's so striking. I've never seen a creature like her."

"I don't think there is one."

Fayne squawked what was obviously a strong agreement. The two girls met eyes and burst into laughter.

Katya's stomach did another somersault, this time with a little flourish at the end.

"I'll get you your usual ale. Ma'am." Lili grinned as she walked away. "I'll be right back."

"Lili?"

The blonde girl stopped and turned, this time in much better humour. "Yes?"

"Would you join me for dinner tonight after you finish work? I haven't had much of a chance to sit and talk to someone like you for a long time."

Katya held her breath as Lili pondered this. Being vulnerable was not one of her strong suits. Today's chat with Athena had a deeper impact than she thought.

Lili smiled her wide smile. "Yes. I'd like that very much." She turned and walked into the café.

Katya exhaled. Fayne was still looking at her, amusement evident in the way she had her head cocked to the side.

"Stop it. Or I'll leave you in the room tonight and you'll miss the date."

A date. Huh. What an unexpected turn of events.

* * * *

A few hours later, Katya and Lili were at the finest restaurant in Fandalore, seated on an outdoor patio overlooking the square where Katya put Fayne through her paces for the children.

Katya had never been to the square at night and was surprised to find it alive with people and entertainment — musicians, jugglers, knife throwers, even a small collection of exotic animals. The square was lit with torchlight, the splashing water in the fountain an appropriate backdrop to the whole thing. As far as appreciating culture went, Katya approved.

Her dinner companion, however, was not as entranced. Lili was looking at the elegant menu, panic-stricken.

"Are you all right, Lili?"

"Umm...can we go somewhere else? I...I can't afford anything here."

Katya smiled in return. "Dinner is my treat, Lili. I asked you, after all."

The girl's blue eyes widened. "Are you sure?"

"Yes. What good is killing lizard men for sacks of gold if you can't enjoy the spoils?" Lili laughed at the echoing of the rumour she had asked Katya about earlier that day.

"Lili, your company is well worth it." She paused, and added, "I assume."

Lili smiled shyly. "Fair enough. You owed me for the 'ma'am' crack from earlier. We're even."

Katya ordered wine, a thirty-year-old vintage made from pears and moon fruit. Since her unfortunate episode over the card game two months ago, she had been careful when it came to the drink. She had no desire to again spiral to the point where she lost control.

Over the wine, they shared stories. Katya talked about her hometown and her parents, about how she had been a good student but hated school and used to skip lessons to spend days on end in the forests around her home, learning about plants, animals and woodcraft. How Shira got tired of watching her spy on his teaching and one day asked her to pick up a blade to learn basic swordplay. How that lesson had turned into five years of teaching, twenty years of adventuring together, and tales of abandoned castles, cursed monasteries and haunted tombs.

Dinner arrived. As they ate, Lili took her turn. "I can't quite compete with all that. Like I said, my life has been very simple. I was born here twenty-four years ago. My father is a blacksmith and my mother is a teacher. She would be appalled that I was having dinner with someone who habitually skipped classes." They both smiled.

Lili took a draw of her wine and went on. "My uncle owns the café where I work. Like I said earlier, I love to read. There aren't that many people my age in town. Most of them move to bigger cities to seek fame and fortune." She stopped to sip her wine again. "That's why I was so…ummm…enthralled, I guess, by you. I hardly know anyone my age…"

"Which I'm not, may I remind you."

Lili laughed. "Fine. Who *looks* my age. Then you come into town wearing beautiful leather armour and bristling with weapons and bringing rumours with you."

Katya's smile in reply was tinged with sadness. "Don't begrudge your life, Lili. There have been many times that I wished I had lived the regular life my parents wanted. Days when sitting in a quiet room looking over business records and planning a family don't sound so bad after all." Katya looked off, lost in thought.

Again. Again, this girl is getting me to share. I hardly know her. What's happening here?

Lili pushed aside her plate and leaned forward. "Katya...I don't know you that well, but obviously something happened that has impacted you beyond just bad memories. Do you...need to talk about it? I get the feeling that there isn't a lot of heart-to-heart time in your world."

Katya stared at Lili, at this insightful, compassionate girl who was giving her the chance to share an incredible burden. Was it fair to weigh her down with something that had caused so much damage in Katya's own life?

No. It wasn't. It would be a tremendous and terrifying thing to dump on someone Katya knew well. For a relative stranger, even someone who seemed as willing to listen as Lili was, it could be a catastrophe. Katya answered her accordingly. "Well, I've been meeting with this witch..."

To the surprise of both, Fayne, who had been sitting on a nearby chair, suddenly squawked and chirped, her tone one of reproach.

Katya sighed. "Fine. You're right."

Lili looked stunned. "Did...she just speak to you?"

"Yes. We understand each other. She told me to stop being foolish and to tell you what happened. Apparently, she thinks you're ready to hear my story."

"I see." Lili looked thoughtful. "Do you agree with her?"

Katya hesitated. "I'm not sure."

Lili reached out and put her hand on top of Katya's, soft and warm on her skin. Clear lacquer glistened on her nails. Katya's hands were callused and rough from years of hitting things and swinging weapons and seldom taking care of herself aside from the basic needs of food, water and shelter. There were stretches of time in Katya's life when a simple hot bath at an inn instead of bathing in a river or pond was a luxury.

Katya was a bit overwhelmed. How could someone so different from her be so compelling?

"I like you, Katya. You're a beautiful, intelligent and worldly elf. I'm sure, given the right circumstances, I could find myself falling in love with you. But you're also an elf who has demons. You don't have to tell me anything, but I think it might be a remarkable thing for both of us if you did."

Katya was speechless. Even Fayne, who was always ready with a sarcastic remark, was silent. "Well. You don't mince words, do you?"

"I've learned there's little sense in doing so. Life is too short to dance around the brambleberry bush. You of all people should understand that."

Katya closed her eyes. Tears welled behind her eyelids, but for the first time since this whole mess had begun, and tears had become a regular part of her life, she didn't hate that they were there.

She met Lili's eyes, wiping away her tears and taking a breath. "Yes, Lili, I have a story. I'll tell you."

Katya did so, over another bottle of wine. The fight at the swamp clearing, the brain scarab and the death of her party. The trek to town and her healing. The trip back to the swamp and the horrible battle with Shira's re-animated body.

How she had lost confidence and locked her weapons away, not wanting to see them. Her descent into blackness for two months, where she had looked for solace through ale and wine. She gave Lili more detail on her drunken encounter with the cheating gamblers and how it had led to Jiris' blunt yet honest assessment that she needed more help than he could provide her.

She talked about how she had spent two more months trying to ignore the nightmares and visions that flooded into her mind and how simple things like the sound of breaking glass or the smell of a stagnant puddle took her back to countless battles from her past. How she was jumpy and fidgety and had to sit with her back to a wall anywhere she went so no one could stand behind her.

She recounted horrible nightmares where she did battle with the re-animated bodies of all her comrades, not just Shira. It was these nightmares that had finally convinced her that she should meet with Athena. Jiris had sworn to Katya that the witch had helped other swordhands who couldn't escape the endless battles of their minds, and Katya agreed at last. She recounted the letter from her brother and talked about her first two visits to Athena and how she left her feeling better, lighter.

She told the human girl everything except for the promise she had made to Shira and what she had done at the lizard men's camp.

The whole time, Lili kept her hand on top of Katya's, squeezing when Katya seemed to be at a difficult part of her tale. She kept holding it even after Katya had finished.

"I don't know what to say, Katya. I have no idea how to even start discussing it with you. The whole thing is completely out of my realm of experience."

Katya turned her hand over and intertwined her fingers with Lili's. She was rewarded with Lili closing her eyes and smiling.

"You don't have to say anything. You listened without judging, and that's enough."

"That may be. But I'd say there are things you need to keep thinking about."

Katya knew that to be true. "Such as?"

Lili moved to a more comfortable position in her chair. "Well, it seems this has all shifted your whole view of the world. For the last twenty years, your answer to almost everything has been rooted in, to be honest, hitting things until they were out of your way. Now you're questioning if that's really an answer. It's violence in the name of a noble cause, but it's violence all the same."

She took a sip of her wine. "It's wrapped up in your past, present and future. I would guess you're wondering about your values, or what you thought were your values. Those are deep questions of thought and spirit that may take years to grapple with."

Katya had never thought that far ahead. She was used to living day to day, never certain the next day was guaranteed. She thought that, after a few sessions with Athena, she would be back on the path she was meant for and would carry on with whatever fate brought her way.

"The thing is, Katya, your brother's letter was right. You've fought every other battle of your life with comrades, with their skills and tools at your back. Why should this be any different just because the battle's taking place in your memories? People will help you if you let them. You don't have to be alone." She squeezed Katya's hand for emphasis.

The elf shook her head. "How did such a young human serving ale to thirsty travellers get so wise?"

Lili smiled her wide smile. "Dad being a blacksmith taught me to swing a hammer. Mom being a teacher taught me to read everything, to question the world and to explore anything intriguing."

She squeezed Katya's hand again. "I don't know about you, but I would love some dessert. The brambleberry pie here is supposed to be…"

On her nearby perch, Fayne stirred. She was watching the square and had seen something that agitated her. Katya let go of Lili's hand and moved to the rail, scanning the square, looking for whatever it was that had alarmed the falcon.

Lili sighed. "I can see spending time with you is going to take getting used to."

Lilli stood and moved to the railing, standing next to Katya, their hips touching. It was a remarkable thing for Katya to be with someone who was so comfortable showing affection and attraction.

"What did Fayne see?"

The bird clucked and whistled.

Katya translated. "She said that big man there, the one wearing all animal skins, was waving a knife around, but he put it away. He's fighting with the woman he's with."

Lili wrinkled her nose in disgust. "Ugh. That's Alog. He claims to be part giant, but most people think he's just an extra-large and unpleasant human. He's a drunk and earns a living by collecting debts people owe to the casinos over in Goldleaf."

"Why doesn't the guard stop him from coming in?"

"Most of them are terrified of him. Depending on who's at the gate, he walks through with no one even talking to him. A guard who tried to stop him from coming in one time ended up with two broken arms and a fractured skull."

"Who's the woman?"

"Not sure. She's whatever unlucky soul caught his eye. He isn't subtle or picky when it comes to choosing who he spends time with. He generally grabs whoever he wants and she becomes his newest companion. Rumour is that he's killed at least two."

"Hmm. You know, when you asked about the nature of evil earlier, I should have mentioned that sometimes, people don't fit any category, they're just..."

Without warning, the brute struck the woman he was with across the face, the force of it knocking her backwards and into the fountain. Around the square, silence descended, broken only by Alog's bellowing laughter.

Katya bristled. She looked over at Fayne, who was having a hard time restraining herself as well.

"Kat."

Katya, startled, turned to look at her.

"Kat? No one ever calls me that."

"It fit the moment. What we talked about earlier? Punching things that are in your way? Sometimes it may be the only alternative. If anyone can answer that with Alog, it's probably you. Go." She leaned over to Katya and kissed her on the cheek. "Do what you have to do."

Katya stood for a moment, partly in shock, partly in amusement, smiling and touching her cheek where Lili had kissed her.

But the smile didn't last long, and as she turned her attention back to Alog, Katya became someone different, instincts and reflexes that had been buried for weeks returning.

A hunter. A predator. A warrior.

"Fayne, stay. I'll be back." She vaulted the railing and jumped to the ground two stories below. On the way down, even amid preparing for combat, Katya realised that, contrary to what she long had believed, she wouldn't necessarily kill anyone besides her family who called her Kat.

The thought made her smile again.

Katya landed on her feet and tumbled forward, taking the force out of the jump. She crossed the square like a giant cat stalking its prey, and many in attendance truly saw for the first time what Katya had been before she wandered into Fandalore.

Katya stopped at the edge of the fountain, where the woman Alog had hit was still floundering in the water. No one had stepped forward to help her. Katya extended her hand and helped the woman out. Katya pointed at one of the jugglers near the fountain.

"You. Please give her your cape. She's freezing."

Hesitating, the juggler stepped forward, undoing the clasp of his cape.

"Stop." Alog had spoken and was now pointing at the juggler. "Unless you plan on learning to juggle with no hands, you put that cape back on."

The man, paralysed by fear, stopped. Katya sighed and walked over to him, taking the cape from his outstretched hand.

"I said stop. That means you too, girl." Alog spoke again, his deep voice and strong presence intimidating everyone in the square.

Except for Katya.

Katya handed the woman the cape. "Go."

"What?" The wet, shivering woman's voice reflected a mix of fear and gratitude.

"Run. Get away from here."

The woman looked at Alog, who, now furious, was stomping towards them.

Katya stepped between the woman and the approaching Alog. "Go, damn it! I'll take care of him. Lose yourself in this town somewhere."

After whispering, "Thank you," the woman did what Katya told her to do and ran.

Alog stopped a few paces from Katya. "That will cost you, girl. I guess you'll be my company for the night in her place."

Katya laughed, a cold and humourless sound. "I don't think so, you overstuffed windbag. Why don't you scurry back to your casinos? Or maybe the cave you and the other trolls live in. You'll save yourself a tremendous amount of both pain and embarrassment."

Red started to creep up Alog's face, starting at his collar. No one had spoken to him like that since he was a child, she guessed. Little mental games to put her opponent off-balance were important in one-on-one fights where she was dealing with a larger opponent who already thought they had an advantage over her. Katya wanted him to be overconfident.

"You're dead, little girl." He closed on her.

This close, Alog was indeed massive. His fists were the size of small hams and, based on how he carried himself, he knew how to swing them. Katya had called him overstuffed to prick at his self-image, but there was muscle under the fat and his legs were strong and sturdy. If he got within grappling distance and grabbed her, she would have to kill him before he could pummel or crush her to death. There were at least a dozen ways she could do so, even with no weapons.

She wasn't even wearing her armour, just a new dark blue bodysuit she had picked up today. Well, the bodysuit would give some protection if he managed to land a punch.

She had chosen the blue because it matched Lili's eyes. Katya hoped she could avoid killing this brute in front of the young human she had been having such a pleasant dinner with.

Alog started their dance as she suspected he would, by throwing a hard right roundhouse punch that whistled through the air.

The first rule of hand-to-hand fighting was simple — the best way to avoid a punch was not to be where it was going to land. Contrary to what most people would do, Katya ducked and stepped closer to him, within the arc of the punch, and jabbed her rigid fingers into the nerve cluster in his right bicep. At the same time, she kicked him with the toe of her boot directly on the shinbone of his left leg.

Her strike made his right arm drop to his side, and his left leg collapsed. When he fell to his knees, the ground near her actually shook with the impact.

Katya didn't want to show it, but jabbing the man's muscle had been like driving her fingers into a tree. Her hand was already aching, and she knew she could strike him like that just one or two more times before she would have to change tactics.

While he was on the ground, she spun around twice, until she was behind him, and kicked him in the back with the sole of her boot, laying him flat on his stomach.

The crowd gasped behind her. Even those who knew Katya by reputation seemed surprised.

"Now, big man, are you going to go back to your casinos with what's left of your dignity?"

Alog pushed himself off the ground with his good arm, then stood. His left leg was shaky but kept him upright.

"You little elfin bitch." He began to walk towards her again. "I was going to kill you quick, but now I think I'll cut you open and lay your guts all over the square for all these nice people to see." With his good hand, he reached down to his boot and removed a long, serrated dagger.

Katya began to back away. "*Elven* bitch."

"What?" Alog looked confused.

"You said elfin. Elfin means small and delicate. I'm elven."

Alog grinned. "Clever. Keep talking. Give us all words to remember you by."

Katya was indeed stalling for time while she planned. The thing Shira had drummed into her about knife fighting was that even the most inexperienced combatant could get one lucky shot in with a blade and the fight would be over. Someone who knew what they were doing with an edged weapon was extremely dangerous. In regular combat she would use her crossbow, or even her staff, and keep him at a distance. She had neither with her.

She looked around the square. About twenty paces to her left was a large cloth target a knife thrower had been using in his performance. Three or four small blades were lodged in the bullseye area. Katya began to circle that way.

Alog continued to close in on her, waving the knife back and forth in front of his face. He looked to his right and noticed the target board before giving another booming laugh. "Do you think those kitchen knives are going to slow me down?" He stopped walking and lifted the shirt he wore, pointing with the tip of the blade to a jagged scar on his chest.

"This was from an Ashruni war axe. The guy who used it ended up getting it back. In his head. So you grab your little blades and see what happens." He let go of his shirt and started moving again.

While he had been talking, Katya had reached the target board. There were four knives, all about the length of her hand. She snatched them from the target and held two in each hand as she turned back to Alog.

"Last chance, big man."

"Yeah. Your last chance." He ran at Katya, moving fast for someone so large.

She flipped two of the blades high into the air and threw the two she still held. One pierced Alog's left bicep, and one went into his right knee. By the time she finished throwing the first two, the others were dropping. She plucked them from the air and launched them as well, one into Alog's other knee, and one into the muscle under his right shoulder blade.

His momentum kept carrying him towards her even as he began to collapse again. In one last display of agility, she sidestepped him, and he ran into the hidden low wall she had manoeuvred herself in front of. With a crash of masonry, Alog hit the wall, taking much of it down to the ground with him.

The silence in the square was broken only by Fayne's triumphant squawk from the restaurant patio. Katya turned to where the bird and Lili were standing. Even from here, Katya could see the look of incredulity on Lili's face. Katya nodded her head and smiled. Lili made a half-wave back, which was about the most she seemed capable of at the moment.

A groan emitted from the large pile of bricks Alog was tangled up in. Taking her time, Katya strolled towards the remains of the wall, feeling the crowd closing in behind her. Quiet murmurs from the assembled group let Katya know that no one had ever seen the ferocious human in such a state.

As she approached, Alog managed to turn his head. "I can't move. What did you do to me, whore?"

Katya clucked her tongue. "Now, that's not nice." She stepped over a few bricks and crouched next to the big human.

"Now it's your turn to listen to me, bloated dungbag. A few months ago, I would have killed you, you mindless brute, and I daresay the world wouldn't miss your presence one bit. Tonight I was nice. What I did was turn off four nerve clusters all at the same time, shutting you down for a little while. Nothing permanent unless I jam those blades in deeper. Meanwhile, you get to live with the hit to your reputation of being beaten down by a little elfin thing. It's tough to extort when you got bested by someone less than half your size."

Somehow, he managed to put a smile on his dust-covered face. "When I can move again, I *will* kill you. It won't even be as quick as gutting you. I'll take my time with you."

Sighing, Katya picked up a brick. "If you want another round, you'll know where to find me. But you're a stubborn man. You need to learn two things. The first is how to treat women."

Alog laughed. The effort of doing so made him cough. "And what's the other?"

"When you've had enough." She reared back her arm before swinging, catching the back of Alog's thick skull with a corner of the brick she held. The impact triggered one more nerve cluster, and the enforcer was out cold. She waited a few seconds to check that he was breathing, then stood and brushed the masonry dust off her bodysuit. She walked over to where the knife thrower stood, mouth agape.

"Thanks for the blades. The balance is good. You probably want to clean them off after they come out of him, though. Could you do me a favour and call for the guards before he wakes up? It'll be a while, but I don't think moving him to the cells will be a quick trip even with a whole squad. Tell them they may want their sleep darts. They'll know what that means."

She smiled, pleased with the fact that something that had taken her down was now going to find new use on someone that she had vanquished in turn. *Things come full circle.*

Katya turned and walked back towards the stairway to the restaurant where Lili and Fayne waited. She had only made it up the first few stairs when someone in the square began clapping. One was soon joined by another, then another, until soon the entire square was full of applauding, cheering townspeople.

Katya stopped and turned around to face the crowd, stunned and not a little embarrassed. In decades of being an Oathtaker, she had seldom received any kind of response, good or bad, from those she had helped. Katya and her comrades didn't do what they did for credit or glory—they did it because they had taken an

Oath to do so. But there hadn't often been any acknowledgement of what Katya had done.

As she stood in front of the crowd, it crossed her mind that stopping the small evils of the world could indeed be a worthwhile endeavour.

However, Katya was not one for the spotlight. Putting Fayne through her paces for a group of children was one thing—being applauded and cheered for fighting was quite another. Not knowing what else to do, Katya waved to the crowd before turning and heading back up to the restaurant.

Much like with her tavern fight, word spread about what happened, and in short order the square was full of people. The proceedings very quickly became a celebration.

Katya climbed the stairs to the patio and found Lili seated again, a full glass of wine in front of her. She was pleased to see Fayne perched on Lili's shoulder.

Katya sat down, poured herself a fresh glass of wine and looked across the table at the blue-eyed girl.

Lili looked back but didn't speak until she had picked up and drained her own glass. "So. That was quite something. You do things like that a lot?"

It was such a ridiculous question under the circumstances that all Katya could do was laugh. "Every now and then, yes."

"I see." Lili refilled her glass. "That was with a bottle of wine in your gullet."

The elf nodded. "It wouldn't be the first time I've fought under those conditions. We used to get challenged by drunks in taverns all the time. Elves have a remarkable tolerance for alcohol, which is why for those two months I was drinking constantly to feel even the slightest effect."

Lili shook her head. "You are the most fascinating person I've ever met."

Katya returned her smile. "Thank you."

The waiter, who had watched Katya in action along with everyone else, brought two large slices of brambleberry pie and two glasses of light, fizzy wine to their table.

"Ladies, these are compliments of the owner. Enjoy." He laid the dessert out on the table. Before he left, he looked down at Katya and held out his hand.

Embarrassed, Katya took it. The waiter squeezed her hand, then let go, before retreating to the kitchen.

Lili had watched this with amusement. "You're not used to adulation."

"No. There was never a lot of accolades in doing what I…what we did."

"Did? Or do?"

Katya looked out over the growing revelry in the square. That was the question she would have to answer to truly move on.

Katya and Lili enjoyed their dessert. The pie was crusty and fruity, and the wine was cold and crisp, a perfect complement to the dessert.

Katya decided it was time to change the subject. "Now, no more serious talk. I get enough questions like that from Athena. Unless you want to end up like poor Alog over there"—she gestured toward the square, where a dozen guards were lifting the unconscious and shackled monster from the brick pile— "no more life-changing questions."

Lili laughed. "I'll take my chances." She reached out and took Katya's hand again. "Now, Kat, the night is young, the wine is cold and I have nothing but time.

Tell me stories of far-off lands and the creatures that live there."

"Hmmm. North, east, south or west?"

"Elf's choice."

"Let's go...north, then? This would be about ten years ago. A group of five of us were stranded at a deep watering hole called the Enlightened Spring. One of the scholars in our group had an old trader's map showing there was a chest at the bottom of the hole, surrounded by poisonous eels. The chest was supposed to contain a cursed gauntlet..."

They talked long into the night. First overlooking the square, until they were gently shooed away from the restaurant, then sitting on the edge of the fountain in the square itself after the crowd had disappeared.

As dawn broke, they sat in silence, alone in the square and watching the sun creep over the buildings on the east side of the city.

"The last time I watched the sun come up, it was so the guards in a castle we were about to storm would be looking right into the light and be blinded."

Lili shook her head. "Of course. Why watch a sunrise just to see something beautiful?"

"Don't mock your elders." Katya stood, pulling Lili up with her. Katya, who was slightly taller, looked down into the girl's eyes. Lili took both of the elf's hands in hers.

"I hope, Kat, that this wasn't a one-time occurrence."

"Do you mean the fight with the drunken casino enforcer or dinner?"

"Dinner. The hand-to-hand combat...well, let's see if it grows on me. If nothing else, it was fun to see another chapter added to the growing legend of Katya Greenleaf."

Katya laughed. "Legend? That's flattering. And, no, as far as I'm concerned, this isn't a one-time happening."

"Good. That makes me happy."

Lili took her hands from Katya's and put them on either side of the elf's face. Reaching up, she kissed Katya softly on the lips. After a few seconds of hesitation, Katya relaxed and returned the kiss.

Lili broke away from her. "You're shaking, Katya. Don't tell me a legendary warrior can't enjoy a kiss."

Katya closed her eyes and turned her face into the sun, tears trickling down her cheekbones. Lili reached up and wiped the tears away with her fingertips.

"I'm one hundred and ten years older than you. I can handle a kiss."

"Then why the trembling? Why the tears?"

Katya smiled with an edge of sadness. "It's not the kiss, Lili. It's the whole night. Being able to feel off guard but still safe. Your understanding. The acceptance from the crowd. All of it."

She looked down into Lili's face. "Because it's been so long since I felt something that nice, and I didn't know if I ever would again."

The blonde girl sighed. "I know. I just wanted you to say it. For your sake, not mine. I want you to remember you can still experience nice things and that you truly aren't alone. Even the darkest night doesn't last forever." Lili leaned in again and kissed Katya on the cheek before backing away from her.

"Good night, lovely elf. I look forward to many more long nights with you."

Katya raised an eyebrow. "Of conversation?"

Lili replied with a roguish grin, "Of whatever. If an old crone like you can keep up with me."

"You're impertinent. Go home, little one."

"Yes, ma'am." She turned to Fayne, who sat dozing on the highest tier of the fountain. "Good night, sweet bird. Get her home safe."

Fayne half opened her eyes before chirping in reply.

Lili faced the elf again. "Good night, Katya Greenleaf. And good morning." With that, she walked out of the square, into the sunlight. Katya watched her until her silhouette faded.

Katya tapped her shoulder and the bird settled on her perch in a rustle of feathers.

"Come on, love. Let's get some rest. We haven't seen the sun come up in quite some time."

Fayne whistled.

"Yes, I get both your meanings. I'm apparently a legend, remember?"

More whistles, punctuated by some twittering came from the bird.

"Yes, she is something special indeed."

Chapter Seven

Six months and three weeks after Day Zero

Lili left work early one afternoon a few days later. It was an unpleasantly warm day, the air hazy and thick with heat. Very few people were out on the streets, preferring the coolness and shade indoors.

She made her way to one of her favourite places in Fandalore – the archives, where she spent considerable time and the archivists knew her by name.

As she had told Katya, Lili read any book or scroll that happened to catch her eye. Growing up with a teacher had given her an appreciation for knowledge of all sorts, from practical to hypothetical.

Today, however, she had a specific topic in mind. The town archive wasn't that large – Lili had heard tales of massive buildings containing thousands upon thousands of books, the thought of which made her heart race – but it had always proven adequate for Lili's needs. She hoped that would be the case again today.

A walk of a few minutes took her to a short, squat building made of dazzling white stone. As usual, there were a few people gathered outside the entrance, enjoying the shade of the overhanging roof. It had only taken Lili one visit to learn that these were fellow knowledge seekers — regular people like her, but with a few scholars and writers thrown into the mix. It was an informal place to gather and share thoughts, ideas, or even engage in the occasional spirited, but always cordial, argument.

When she had time, Lili joined the group, but today she greeted those that she knew and proceeded inside.

Lili was always struck by the quiet in the building. Even on the busiest days on the street outside, the noise never made its way through the walls. It gave the air a sense of flatness, but Lili had quite come to enjoy the drastic difference inside. It was like entering into another world.

Which, she supposed, was a fair comparison. This building contained the means to take one back in time, to the other side of the world, even to the future. It provided her with an escape when the walls of the café or of her bedroom seemed to be closing in on her.

The archive building was circular. In the middle were a few tables and comfortable chairs for those who preferred to peruse books or scrolls there instead of taking things home. There were also a few desks for serious scholars who couldn't imagine doing research from a padded chair.

At the back of the circle was a desk, and behind that desk sat Altheasus, one of the most intelligent people Lili, in her admittedly limited experience, had ever met. He was the head archivist, responsible for overseeing the many shelves of reading material, as well as the junior archivists whose job it was to collect, restore and maintain the books and scrolls lining the shelves around the outside of the circle.

The building itself was deceptive, Lili knew. While the shelves in the circle were full, in some cases groaning under the weight of books, there was also a sizeable room underground that contained more valuable materials, offices and workrooms, and, some said, a special locked room where things considered a bit too arcane or shocking for general consumption were tucked away.

Altheasus, a tall, almost gaunt man, sat in his usual spot behind the main desk. Despite his severe appearance and full set of scholar's robes, which he wore despite the heat of the day, Lili had found him to have a dry sense of humour and an honest admiration for those who came into his domain looking for knowledge.

He looked up from what he was studying and smiled. "Lili, my dear girl. How wonderful to see you."

Lili smiled in return. "Good afternoon, Altheasus. It's far too hot to do much more today than sit down with a stack of books."

"I would argue that was a fine activity for any day, but I take your meaning." He reached for a thick leather journal, which Lili knew from long experience to be a sort of catalogue of books and scrolls in the archive building.

"Now, are you here for your usual mix of topics or is there something specific you had in mind?"

"Specific."

He raised an eyebrow. "I was wondering how long it would take you."

Lili was confused. "I...don't understand."

"Archivists make it a point to collect information of all kinds, dear girl. It's no secret who you've been keeping company with, nor is it a secret that she has a unique…history, shall we say?"

Lili flushed to the roots of her hair.

"My dear, please don't take that as judgement or gossip, just fact. Rest assured that you are not the first person who has come to me seeking information on the Blood Oath, the Oathtakers or the Three. Or even Katya herself."

"I see. I suppose I'm not surprised."

"In fact, so many people have been asking that I've taken what we have in our collection out of circulation and made them available here in the archive itself." He gestured to a neat stack of four books sitting on the corner of his desk.

"Someone returned these to me not an hour ago. They're available for your use." He slid the books to Lili. "I don't know if you'll find the answers you're looking for. In fact, you may know more than some of these books, considering that you are…friends, I suppose? Yes, that will do. Friends with an actual Oathkeeper."

Lili again flushed furiously.

"Perhaps you can convince our fine elf to write a book of her own. Oh, that would be marvellous!" He clapped his hands together at the thought of it. "No one has ever found anything substantial left in writing by an actual Oathtaker. As you'll see, they are quite a close-mouthed group in general. The nature of what they do, I suppose. Still, one can hope…"

"I'll suggest it." Lili's flush had faded, leaving only a trace of warmth in her cheeks.

"Oh, please do. Now, off to a desk with you. As always, I'm here for anything you may need."

"Thank you." Lili took the stack of books and went to the collection of chairs in the middle, all of which were blessedly empty.

She dropped the books onto a table then slumped into a chair, needing some time to compose herself. Her unexpected exchange with the archivist had left her heart racing, as well as her mind. While Lili had never been a private person, finding out that her acquaintance with Katya was public knowledge rattled her a bit.

She would have to raise the topic with Kat at dinner tonight.

Looking to regain some balance, she turned to the books, deciding to start with the slimmest one first.

It turned out to be an overview of the trading market, a few years old, listing the major commerce houses large enough to do business across the continent.

Lili turned to one well-read page, which said across the top, "Greenleaf Spice Traders." The entry on Katya's family company didn't include much beyond what Lili already knew. The trading house was in its third generation of being operated by a Greenleaf. Katya's brother Elias specialised in spices both exotic and common, and maintained not only a large collection of sales houses across the continent, but also a large fleet of ships that ventured far and wide in search of new wares.

She set that book aside and moved onto the next, a thicker book bound with burgundy leather bearing the title *Guilds of Nakall*. The book covered exactly what it said, discussing the various professional guilds across the continent.

Lili flipped through the text, skipping sections that held no interest for her and stopping to read when some titbit of information caught her eye. In less than an hour, she had made her way through sections on merchants, craftsmen, entertainers, healers, jurists, food and drink vendors and farmers.

Upon reaching the final chapter, she found the information that appeared to make the book so popular, a chapter titled "Dark Guilds."

The title was exciting, she had to admit, yet also a bit frightening.

She started reading.

In addition to the more respectable guilds detailed in this tome, there also exist in Nakall several groups that, while they technically meet the definition of a guild, specialise in practices far more sinister.

Very little information is to be had on these guilds, given the secretive nature of their activities. Their members are not willing to providing audiences to scholars, often on pain of death, and most efforts to infiltrate their ranks have ended in injury, torture, murder or some combination.

However, the authors of this volume are confident in stating that there exist in Nakall guilds dedicated to the following darker arts and skills: thievery, crooked gaming and gambling, poisonings, black market goods, slavery, unnatural medical practices (grave-robbing, sales of various body parts, necromancy), and assassination.

There also exists a guild which, while professing to be acting in the name of 'good' and 'lawfulness', engages in many of the above practices. Unlike these other guilds, however, their members do not dwell only in the shadows but wear their hearts upon their sleeves, recognisable by what their members call a 'Mark of the Blood Oath.'

These 'Oathtakers', as they are named, are, in the opinion of these authors, of even worse character than those of other dark guilds. While the other dark guilds act in the name of their chosen professions, wretched as they may be, they are at least doing so under no pretences. 'Oathtakers' hypocritically utilise many of these same activities in the pursuit of 'justice', as determined by themselves. In our experience, justice is subjective.

Somehow, these warriors, whose total numbers are not known, have convinced the public at large that they are bastions of light in a world full of darkness and that their ranks are the last line of defence if the many hells should someday spew forth all manner of unholy beasts.

Lili closed the book and slumped back in the chair. She had not expected to read such harsh criticism of the order that Katya had dedicated her life to. Like most other people, she absolutely believed that those who had sworn their Oath were a force for good against those who would harm others.

She sighed. She had known that digging into Katya's life would produce a lot of grey and very little black and white, but she hadn't expected to be off to such a jarring start.

She picked up the next book, bound in black leather, the cover of which had no decoration, not even a title. It took a few pages before she reached the title, *Secret Sects and Societies*, and the names of the authors, who described themselves as "Messrs. Lion, Eagle and Tiger."

Lili was not surprised. Poking around into the business of groups who wanted to stay in the shadows could be a quick end to an academic career.

Lili smiled. This volume held some promise.

Like with the previous book, she skimmed through until she found the section she wanted.

THE COUNCIL OF THE BLOOD OATH

The Council of the Blood Oath is an anomaly compared to many of the groups in this volume, in that, while the inner workings of the Council are shrouded in mystery, the goals of the Council and the members dedicated to carrying out those goals are publicly known. Indeed, the members of the Council make themselves targets by agreeing to be marked with a brand or tattoo (accounts differ).

There was an illustration of the Oathtaker Mark on the page following, exactly like Kat's.

While it is difficult to pinpoint how the Council of the Blood Oath operates, based on the observations of many scholars, some broad assumptions can be made.

The information that does exist about the history of the Council shows that it has been in existence for at least hundreds of years, if not longer. It is very likely the Council is older, but no written records can verify this.

There are three senior members of the Council, referred to as 'The Three', who appear to be tasked with making decisions that impact the Council of Oathtakers as a whole, and are also responsible for initiating new members

It would appear members of any and all races are accepted as Oathtakers, save for those who have no redeeming qualities (ex. lizard men), sense of nobility (ex. races of dark magic) or adequate intelligence (ex. animals and insects).

Oathtakers are only considered for membership based on the recommendations of current Oathtakers, quite often coming from a mentor / mentee relationship.

Lili nodded. That was how Katya had been accepted, after many years of learning with Shira. She read on.

New Oathtakers are initiated into the fold at a secret ceremony, which, despite occurring for hundreds of years, has never been documented aside from some oral history, and even that information is questionable. It is quite likely that the location of these ceremonies is shielded by substantial magic use on top of the built-in confidentiality the Oathtakers are no doubt sworn to.

The Council appears to be self-funded, as no formal governments or organisations have ever admitted to providing the Council with any resources or support. While there are instances of Oathtakers being compensated for undertaking specific missions for a town council or village elders, we have not been able to find any ongoing connections. Individual Oathtakers seem to operate by an unknown and complex process of retaining goods and wealth they find from those they dispatch, which appears to fund their ongoing crusade.

Katya had told Lili about the way that she and her various companions over the years collected items and valuables from fallen enemies as well as fallen comrades. This ensured that not only did Oathtakers always have the means to maintain their way of life, but also that the families of any Oathtakers who died as part of their fight would be taken care of.

She turned back to the book to read the remaining section.

As stated earlier, Oathkeepers make no secret of what it is they do, bearing bright-red symbols of their allegiance on their skin. There is no reason to assume that Oathkeepers do not have friends and family whom they leave behind when they take up their mission. Presumably these same friends and family could then become a liability to the Oathkeepers they are attached to. With this in mind, we can state with great confidence that there is a subset of members of the Council (accounts state older members or those who develop some type of infirmity) whose responsibility it is to watch over those friends and family while their loved ones are adventuring around the continent. To cross the family of an Oathkeeper seems a sure way to court death

Although we could speculate even further about this mysterious Council of Oathkeepers, our goal is to avoid travelling too far into the realm of gossip, which is plentiful. For now, we will say that this Council is perhaps the most unusual of those in this tome, as it has a very public face while having a body and brain that remain firmly in the shadows. We will leave judgements on the propriety of what the Oathtakers do to our esteemed readers.

Lili closed the leather covered book and put it onto the stack of the others she had read. The last in the stack turned out to be a simple book called *Of War and Warriors*, containing chapters on military tactics, weapons, armour, and famous battles throughout Nakall's existence. There were a few mentions of Oathtakers, but nothing substantial, and in fact less than Lili knew herself from storytelling sessions with Kat.

The blonde girl stood and stretched, feeling the effects of spending a few hours sitting, even in a chair as comfortable as the one she had been using. She returned the books to Altheasus and bade him farewell before heading back onto the street.

In the time she had been inside, the sun had sunk below the horizon, bringing some welcome coolness in its wake. Even with the setting sun, the light outside was still dazzling after the dimmer torchlight of the archives, and it took her vision a moment to clear.

She reminded herself to start using Kat's trick of letting her eyes slowly adjust to bright light instead of overwhelming them.

When she stopped seeing spots, she moved out into the street, heading for Katya's inn, where she was meeting her elf for dinner.

As she walked, she let what she had read roll through her mind. To say it was mixed messaging was an understatement. Katya had told her quite a bit about the Council, some of which lined up with the book on guilds and other bits which lined up with the secret society tome.

She sighed. As with many things, she supposed, the truth was somewhere in the middle. History was written by the winners, and opinion was subjective.

If nothing else, she had new food for thought about Katya's background, and felt like she had more perspective to help her put herself into Katya's boots. Just because she would never be a warrior herself didn't mean she couldn't do her best to understand the warrior's mindset.

Still, at the back of her mind, some of what she read lingered, nagging at her.

'Self-righteous.'

'Hypocritical.'

'Make themselves targets.'

'Convinced the public they were bastions of light.'

'Firmly in the shadows.'

She sighed again. It looked like tonight's dinner topic was set. Lili hoped she was ready to hear the other side of what she had spent her afternoon learning.

Chapter Eight

Seven months after Day Zero

Lili was sitting on the edge of Katya's bed. It was an unusual experience, waiting for the elf, as Katya was normally ready to head out to wherever their adventures of the day would take them.

Today, though, Fayne had been out on a flight to stretch her wings. Somehow, she had ended up tangling with a barbed frog that she had no doubt seen as an easy snack. Instead, the frog had shot the arrow-like quills from its back into Fayne's wing.

She had made it back to Katya's rooms, although her landing was hardly graceful, and she was in quite a bit of pain from a mild poison on the barbs.

When Lili arrived, Katya was in the bathroom with her bird, working on removing the barbs with tools from a small medical kit. Katya had scrubbed Fayne with cleaner and water to remove any trace of the poison that might be on her feathers, and when Lili saw the falcon, she couldn't stop herself from laughing at its bedraggled appearance. She was met with a string of bird profanity and Katya suggested she wait in the main room while she finished. Lili agreed, gave Katya a quick peck on the cheek and apologised to Fayne, who seemed to accept.

With nothing else to do, Lili let her gaze wander around the room when she noticed, for the first time she could remember, that the storage cabinet attached to the wall was unlocked and open. She knew that Katya secured armour, weapons and tools in the cabinet. She must have retrieved the medical kit from there to treat Fayne.

Lili had never seen any of Katya's equipment up close. Even when they went wandering through the woods near Fandalore, the elf carried a simple pack holding basic equipment like rope, some medicines and a water skin. The only weapons she carried on their outings were a dagger and her staff. While Katya had mentioned her crossbow and sword while storytelling, she had never shown them to Lili.

Exceedingly curious about this still secretive aspect of Katya's life, she realised this was an ideal opportunity.

"Kat?"

"Yes?" Her voice was agitated, no doubt due to having to wrestle barbs out of a feisty bird, no matter how tame Fayne was.

"Can I take a look in your cabinet?"

There was no immediate answer. After a moment, she replied, but with hesitation in her voice. "Sure. But be careful. There are some things in there that could cut you to the bone before you know it."

"Of course."

Excited, Lili crossed the floor to the storage cabinet. She opened the door and was pleased to find that a simple lantern turned on when she did so.

Hanging in the cabinet were several amazing things. In Lili's mind, each was more fascinating than the last.

She started with Katya's armour. It came in two pieces, both sleek black leather—a chest plate and leggings. The only thing that stood out from the jet-black material, aside from a few duller spots that Lili knew to be giant rat blood, was a small green emerald representing Katya's bloodline crest, mounted on the leather.

When Lili looked closer, she could see a few spots where the armour had been repaired. Lili was no armourer, not even a seamstress, but it was obvious that the repairs had been done by masters of their trade.

Lili knew that Katya had had the armour custom-made, designing it herself to be a variation of the suit a thief would use—light and flexible, lots of storage and colouring to blend into the darkness of night or shadow. It wasn't traditional battlefield armour, but it wasn't meant to be, and it suited Katya's acrobatic combat style.

The chest piece was made of dozens of diagonal strips of leather with extra padding at the shoulders and waist. Thinner leather sleeves were sewn to the chest plate. Lili squeezed one of the sleeves and found that while it was extremely soft, the material was braced by hidden metal strips that would assist with blocking strikes.

A separate pair of leather leggings hung next to the chest plate. They extended far enough down the elf's legs to be tucked into the tall leather boots Katya always wore.

Both the chest piece and leggings bore many pockets which held the small tools Katya needed often — lockpicks, medicines, poisons, fire starters, bribery gold, treats for Fayne. Lili guessed that, if she started digging, she would eventually find many more pockets that were hidden.

Katya had told her stories of tracking down healers, armourers and mages who had added special enchantments to the armour for her, enchantments that were only active when the armour detected Katya's aura. When the elf wore the chest plate, she had extra resistance to heat and cold, increased stamina, decreased visibility, even some simple pain-killing magic that would get her through the minor wounds and damage of battle without needing to stop and apply medicine. It would be fascinating to see the enchantments. It was possible, but it took substantial experience as a mage to do so.

Lili itched to try the chest plate on but sighed in resignation. Despite her trim figure, she was curvier than Katya and knew that the elf's armour would be a snug fit. Magically changing size was something the armour couldn't do.

She moved on to the beautiful crossbow called the Last Whisper. In Lili's eyes, it was as much art as weapon. The grip and stock were made of polished onyx wood, while dragon bone formed the limbs. She ran a finger over the bone. She'd never touched such an exotic material before.

Small etchings on bronze panels inlaid into the stock told the story of the first owner of the weapon, a wealthy tyrant whose name had been lost to the sands of time. It had cost the elf no small amount of gold to have several mages study the crossbow to coax out all its secrets, and she had told Lili she was convinced that even now there were aspects to the weapon still hidden away.

Finally, she moved on to the longsword. Katya had told her it was named in a language from the other side of the great oceans. She couldn't speak the language but had learned it was called Isshogai, which meant "For Life" in the common tongue.

Lili didn't understand the conventions of naming a weapon, but it struck her as odd that something forged to kill bore a name that evoked images of birth and long life.

Katya had told her the sword was enchanted to be vicious when fighting undead things. Could that have something to do with it?

Lili could also rationalise that the name meant lives were saved using the weapon, but that led to all sorts of uncomfortable questions. What if someone considered evil was wielding the sword? What if it was used in anger for a personal grudge? Did the name really mean anything?

Regardless of its beauty and utility, much like her reading of the week before, the sword left Lili with an uneasy feeling about the death that this weapon had brought to the world.

Despite herself, Lili was curious about the weapon's practical aspects. She picked it up, the blade sheathed in the scabbard, and held it in one hand. It was incredibly light for such a large weapon. Lili pulled the blade from its guard. She examined the section of blade she had exposed and was surprised to find it free of marks or scratches. She had assumed that a weapon that Katya had been using for years would show signs of wear, of many battles fought. Lili guessed there must be some enchantment that kept it sharp and maintained.

She withdrew the sword the rest of the way and hung the scabbard back up. Lili had played games of knights and dragons with wooden swords when she was younger, but she had never held an actual combat weapon. Cautious of the blade's sharpness, she held the sword away from her body, giving it a few experimental swings.

Even given her reservations about the weapon, Lili had to admit that it was very natural to move the sword. The handle had an unexpected warmth – she had expected the metal to be cold to the touch.

She pulled the blade closer to her body, then lifted it over her head parallel to the ground, like she was blocking a strike coming from above. She repeated the motion, this time taking a step backwards as if moving away from an opponent.

"Very nice."

Startled, Lili turned around to see Katya leaning in the doorway of the bathroom, Fayne perched on her shoulder.

Lili blushed. "How long have you been watching?"

"Long enough to see that you move pretty well with that in your hand."

"It feels amazing. Like it was made…"

"Like it was made for you? Yes, that's one of the signs of the work of a master bladesmith. Anyone can pick it up and feel like it was custom built for them."

Katya moved over to where Lili stood. "Turn around and face the cabinet."

Lili did so.

"Hold on to the handle with both hands and pull it into your body. It will feel odd at first, but put your right hand against the guard and tuck your left underneath it."

As she did so, Katya stepped behind Lili, wrapping her arms around the girl and placing her hands on top of Lili's. "Let me guide you through a few things."

Lili smirked.

"You're being impertinent again. Just work with me."

For the next few minutes, Katya guided Lili through basic cuts, thrusts and parries. Their bodies were in contact the whole time, Katya's upper body moving in sync with Lili's.

Finally, Katya released her grip and stepped back. Both girl and elf were flushed, and not just from exertion.

Lili spoke first. "That was surprisingly…intimate. Thank you." She seemed to be having trouble catching her breath.

"You're a good student. Good hands."

Lili raised an eyebrow and again smirked. Katya rolled her eyes and they both laughed.

Katya took the blade from Lili and replaced it in the scabbard. She hung the sword up, then checked the rest of the contents of the cabinet. Finding everything to her satisfaction, and happy at having been able to share this part of her life with the girl she was falling in love with, she locked the cabinet and turned back into the room.

"So," the elf said, "where are we off to…?"

Much to her shock, in the time Katya had taken to re-secure the cabinet, Lili had stripped off her clothes and slipped under the covers of Katya's bed, her lovely curves visible under the sheets.

"Oh." It was all Katya could manage.

Lili blushed again. "Umm...why don't we stay here today?" Her voice held an alluring mix of shyness and anticipation, as if she couldn't quite believe her own actions. She moved the sheets next to her back and patted the bed. "Join me?"

Katya's stomach was doing somersaults. She hadn't expected such a bold action from the human girl but was thrilled with the development. She had known it was only a matter of time until she and Lili became lovers, but she hadn't expected it would happen this way.

She reached behind her back and undid the closure of the bodysuit she wore, letting it fall to the floor. As it fell, she felt an unfamiliar combination of vulnerability and comfort.

Lili took in Katya's body. The elf was fit and muscular, but she had the inevitable scars and marks of combat on her skin.

"You look pretty good for an old crone."

Katya grinned. "Old crones can teach young ones some interesting tricks."

Lili replied, very simply, "I'm ready to learn."

Katya's stomach did another set of flips.

She slid under the sheets next to Lili, losing herself in the girl's sparkling blue eyes and gentle touch.

* * * *

Over the next few weeks, Katya got used to the rhythm of being in a relationship that didn't involve constantly having to save a partner from whatever threat lay around the corner. She and Lili spent most days together, exploring Lili's favourite places in Fandalore—coffee houses, shops, even the archive. Much to Lili's amusement, during their visit to the latter, the gaunt old archivist Altheasus had been as giddy as a child, relishing the opportunity to ask questions of an actual Oathtaker.

They dined together a few times with Lili's parents. Katya was charmed by Lili's simple but comfortable home, filled with touches of both academia and metalworking. Lili's father Rowan was very skilled for a non-magical blacksmith, and his creations of shelves, tables, chairs and cabinets formed much of the structure of the home. Her mother, Stella, used her husband's craft to good effect.

During one dinner visit, Lili had been asked by her mother to run to the local grocer for a forgotten spice necessary for the stew that was being prepared. The girl was slightly panic-stricken at leaving Katya alone, but her elf gave her a reassuring nod.

It had taken Lili longer than expected as the grocer closest to her house had not had the laceflower she was looking for, necessitating a trip to one a few blocks away. She did not quite run home, but it was close.

As she neared her house, Katya and her father were in the small yard between his shop and the house itself. Lili stopped, curious as to why they were there.

She ducked down a side alley that would allow her to get next to the yard without being seen, as a large hedge separated the two. Keeping in mind Katya's excellent hearing, she crept along the road, stopping next to where her father and girlfriend stood.

"What's this vintage called?"

Lili frowned. Were they drinking?

Her father answered, "Donkey's Kick."

"It's accurate. I haven't had a whisky with this body in years. It adds to the cigar."

A few seconds later, a fragrant, some might say acrid, cloud of smoke rose from the other side of the hedge.

Lili was incredulous. On top of the whisky, they both appeared to be smoking the pungent cigars her mother had forbade her father from indulging in unless he was outside.

Her father spoke again. "Where were we?"

"I was telling you that I thought it was madness to not have silver bound into any weapon that you wanted to use against the undead."

Rowan drew at his cigar. "What about fespyx? It's already hewn off from silver veins. Just as good."

"Fespyx? Just as good if you want some ghoul chomping your arm off because your first swing didn't kill it. You might as well just use prelium."

"Ha! Prelium is a perfectly good metal for arrowheads and shields, I'll have you know…"

Having heard enough, and shaking her head at yet another layer of Katya's ability to adapt to just about anything, she headed back to her road and came up the walk like she had come directly from the grocer.

She took the spice to her mother. "Where's Kat?"

"Oh, your father wanted to show off his shop. They're out there somewhere." She stirred the spice into the large pot over the fire. "Could you tell both of them to come inside?"

Lili opened the back door and repeated her mother's request loudly enough so that Katya and her father could hear her from where they were, around the corner of the house.

A few seconds later, both appeared with empty hands, mugs and cigars vanished.

"Did you get the spice your mother needed, Lil?"

"I did. She's dishing the stew up now."

"Wonderful." Her father stopped to give her a peck on the cheek as he passed her.

Lili, doing her best to maintain a straight face, held the door open for Kat.

"Did you like Dad's shop?"

"It was great. Very complete." She leaned in to kiss the other cheek. As she did, she whispered, "It's rude to eavesdrop, you know."

Lili's eyes widened, and Katya, now the straight-faced one, walked into the kitchen.

* * * *

Another time, Lili's mother had asked Katya to join her and Lili, for tea, 'just the girls', as she put it. Katya was hardly one to indulge in girl's time, but Katya knew that accepting Lili also meant, at least to an extent, accepting her family.

As a teacher, Stella was fascinated by Katya's stories of her travels. As she poured tea, she regaled Katya with questions about various places and things across Nakall.

Katya patiently answered. Lili had heard most of it before, and Katya noticed that the girl seemed more intent on watching the interaction between her mother and her than any information Katya was providing.

After an hour or so, the question Katya had been waiting for finally came up.

"So, Katya. With this exciting life you've led, you must not have had much time for school."

Lili smiled, somewhat smugly in Katya's opinion, as she had all but assured Katya this topic would come up.

Katya decided there was no point in dancing around it. "To be honest, no. I don't begrudge anyone who sticks with school, but it just wasn't for me. My classrooms were the woods, hills and caves around my house."

"I see." Stella pursed her lips in obvious distaste. "But don't you feel like you missed out on so many things that would help you in what you do now?"

Katya smiled. It wasn't that she enjoyed arguing, but, at its core, it was just another form of combat. Fencing with words wasn't as dangerous, but it could certainly be as challenging.

"Well...I learned history from crawling through dozens of old castles, tombs and libraries. I learned about plant and animal life when I was taught about medicines and poisons. I've seen more of Nakall than most people ever will from a textbook. I've come across beautiful works of art and literature and been able to study them up close."

She sipped her tea. "Metallurgy. Anatomy. Botany. Biology. Navigation. Economics. Geology. Negotiating. All things I've learned about through my years as an Oathkeeper. And all things it would have taken me years of sitting in a classroom to experience." She sat back, waiting for the reply.

While Lili's mother furiously stirred her tea in an apparent effort to plan her answer, Katya spared a moment to glance at Lili. The blonde girl had a straight face, but winked at Katya in support.

After a few seconds, Stella stopped her aggressive stirring. She opened her mouth to reply, appeared to think better of what she was going to say, and stayed silent. A few seconds more passed before she said, "Well, I just hope that by the time grandchildren come along, you'll have changed your perspective."

Lili sighed. "Mom…"

"Oh, Lili, let a mother dream." She picked up a plate of scones and offered it to Katya. "Would you like one, Katya? They're home baked. Did you learn any baking while you were crawling through swamps?"

"Mother." Lili said it with a harsher edge this time, indicating that the matter was over.

"Of course, dear." The conversation returned to less touchy subjects.

* * * *

An hour later, elf and girl were making their way to Katya's rooms at the inn.

"I'm so sorry, Kat."

"Don't be silly. She's your mom and she has your best interests at heart."

"I know, but, still…"

Katya laughed. "Do you know what an ice tiger is?"

"No."

"It's in the big cat family. There are none around here. They're a northern creature. They have an interesting habit, though. When they have a litter of young, they'll pretend to be very gentle, very giving. They'll even turn their back on the kittens sometimes."

Lili furrowed her brow. "Why would they do that?"

Katya smiled. "It's a trap. They wait for a predator to take advantage of what appears to be weakness. As soon as whatever it is gets within attack distance, the ice tiger pounces and kills the predator in a brutal show of force."

"That's awful."

"Yes, but it's also a message. Don't dare consider hurting my children."

Lili stopped and looked up at Katya. "Wait…are you saying my mom is an ice tiger?"

"If tigers drank tea, yes."

Lili could do nothing but stare, before bursting into laughter that continued the rest of their walk.

Lili introduced Katya to her small circle of friends, young adults who had decided to stay in Fandalore instead of striking out for a larger city. Katya gave it an honest effort, but often couldn't participate in their conversations about town gossip, clothing, travelling minstrels or poor working conditions at their jobs, having no frame of reference for doing so. Katya had once tried to change the topic of conversation to the best way to skin and prepare various wild creatures for meat, but the alarmed eyes of Lili's friends quickly put an end to her effort.

One day, their gossip became so tedious that Katya wished that some undead creature would come shambling into the town square so she would have something to do. Lili, noticing her clear discomfort, used a break in the conversation to pass Katya a note.

Kat, I know this is very difficult for you, but I love you for trying to make this part of my life part of yours as well. How about I make it up to you tonight by starting at your surprisingly cute elven toes and working my way up your body with kisses? When I get to your lips, let's see what happens.

Katya's stomach dropped a few notches. Flushing, she looked across the table at Lili, who was wearing a sly grin and raised her eyebrows inquisitively.

"That will be fine, yes." Katya, who had grown very warm despite the coolness of the evening, drained her goblet of ale in one go.

Lili did, however, still have to work. Although Katya's various stashes of loot could cover the costs of anything they wanted to do, Lili did have familial obligations to work at the café. Katya respected that.

As a result, she found herself with a few free days a week. She often exercised in her rooms, even ran through combat manoeuvres as best she could, but there was simply not enough space.

Pondering this problem one day while standing at the window watching Fayne do loops and rolls high in the air, her gaze wandered to the stables below. There were three stalls there, meant for horses or other mounts. In all the time she had been there, she had never seen an animal lodged.

After a very quick conversation with the dwarven innkeeper, in which several coins changed hands, Katya was the new renter of all three stalls.

By the next morning, both Lili's father and a woodcrafter he recommended were at the stables, removing walls and building racks, targets, and several life-sized training dummies to Katya's specifications. Within a few hours, she was joyfully swinging her weapons in the open air, able to simulate combat strikes without fear of damage to anything breakable.

The third time she was using her new training yard, it became apparent that she was being watched. Katya had long ago learned to split focus between tasks, and every few seconds while she was working with her staff, she spotted a mop of brown hair around the corner of the stable wall.

Finally, she struck the training dummy one fierce blow, kept the staff in place and said, without looking around "You can come out. It's all right."

By the time she had turned, a girl, a decade or so younger than Lili, had stepped from behind the wall. Her clothes and face were streaked with dirt, but bright and curious brown eyes took in everything about Katya and the stables.

Katya smiled. "Are you lost, little one?"

"No, not lost."

"Shouldn't you be in school, then?"

"Well…my father *thinks* I'm at school."

Katya had to work to suppress her widening grin. "I see. And your mother?"

The girl rolled her eyes as only young girls could and sighed. "School is *so* boring. My father says I should go, but Mother says on beautiful days like this I'll learn more from exploring what's out in the world, as long as I don't leave the city walls."

Katya leaned against the stall. "Your mother sounds like a smart woman." She ran her gaze up and down the girl's body. "It looks to me like you may have explored a pig pen or two today."

The girl looked down at her clothing. "Yeah, I guess I'm a bit dirty. But I found some lovely tunnels by the water pumping station. It was pretty muddy." She stopped to reach into a pocket, digging for something. "But I found this." She held up a filthy coin with considerable pride.

Katya smiled again. "May I see it?"

The girl deftly flipped it to Katya, who snatched it out of the air as smoothly. She rubbed away a layer of grime with her thumb. It wasn't an old coin, not by

Oathtaker standards, but it had lain in the mud for some time and must have taken some work to retrieve.

She liked this girl.

"Do you have a name, explorer?" She handed the coin back.

"Well, my full name is Jaygon, but everyone calls me Jay."

Katya nodded. "Jay it is, then." She nodded towards her staff, standing in the crook of two walls. "Tell me, Jay, have you ever held a staff?"

The girl's eyes lit up. "No. Never."

"I'll make you a deal. You go home, clean up and ask your parents. If they agree, I'll start teaching you different ways to take care of yourself and maybe some things about exploring the world." She held up a finger. "But it will only be *after* school, all right?"

Jay, by now wearing a broad smile, excitedly shook her head.

Katya considered for a moment. "If you have two or three friends who would like to learn with you, you can bring them, but the same deal goes — after school and their parents must say yes."

"Sure." Jay was practically vibrating with excitement.

"If your parents want to meet me, they can find me here."

"Alright." Jay held out the coin. "Is this enough to pay you?"

Katya was suddenly overcome by a wave of sadness. The conversation, right down to offering what little money she had, reminded her of the day that Shira had grown tired of watching her peek at his training sessions and asked her to participate.

The elf's smile was bittersweet. "You keep your coins, explorer. I'm happy to teach you and your friends." She pointed to the stable gate. "Now, off with you. Be here tomorrow after school and we'll start."

The girl scurried for the gate, but stopped a few steps short and turned back. "I'm sorry...I don't know what to call you. We call our teachers Miss or Sir..."

"Katya will be fine, Jay. No need for Miss."

"Katya." The girl said it like the elf was a priceless work of art, then headed out of the stables through the gate.

Katya retrieved her staff and began her exercises again. Lili would no doubt have one of the impertinent comments and faces she made when Katya did something that was decidedly un-warrior-like ready when she told her about this new idea of mentoring these girls...

But was it? Wasn't teaching a new generation her skills and passing on knowledge part of the circle of being a warrior? An Oathtaker?

Katya decided it was indeed, and as she struck the head of the training dummy, Katya thought she might keep this new adventure to herself.

For now, anyway.

Chapter Nine

Eight months after Day Zero

Katya was again facing Shira's re-animated corpse. The lich had taken over his body and was closing in on her, swinging the great battle-axe in wide sweeps. This time, however, the lich had taken the time to attach the plated helmet to the rest of the armour with ice, welding it into place, and had covered the damaged chest plate with a sheet of ice, adding another layer of protection from Katya's weapons.

The creature had learned a few tricks after Katya had killed it several times.

Katya moved backwards, trying to create time to draw her sword, but both her arms and legs were leaden, like she was moving through quicksand.

She heard more lich wails from behind her. She forced her body to turn and was confronted with the rest of her deceased party, all of them showing the same sickly yellow eyes that Shira had. They were swinging various weapons or preparing to fire arrows at her.

Two of the mages who had travelled with them were readying spells, their hands beginning to glow with building energy.

A noise to her left drew her attention. Coming towards her through the swamp were dozens of sets of glowing yellow eyes—the eyes of a huge group of lizard men approaching her through the haze... The lizard men she had slaughtered at their encampment.

"Kat." The voice was behind her.

She spun the other way. Her brother now stood between her and Shira's possessed body. He carried no weapons and wore no armour, but was dressed in the usual stylish tunic he wore every day. Around his neck, he bore on a gold chain a twin to the green emerald leaf Katya wore on her armour.

Over his shoulder, Katya could see more yellow eyes approaching. They were vastly outnumbered and would be even if several other Oathtakers were with her.

"Elias? What the hell are you doing?"

"I'm helping you, Kat. You can't do this alone."

"You'll get killed."

He gestured around at the closing circle of foes. "You won't?"

"If I do, I'll go down fighting."

Her brother smiled sadly. "Kat, you still haven't learned. You don't always have to fight. Not fighting something anymore doesn't mean you're giving in."

Elias turned and stood in front of Shira's body. He put his arms out to the side, showing he was no threat. He looked at his sister over his shoulder.

"Goodbye, Kat."

Before she could reply, the blade of Shira's axe burst from Elias' back, and just as suddenly withdrew. Her brother's body crumpled to the ground.

"No!" Katya tried to move, to run, to do anything, and couldn't.

The possessed Shira stepped over her brother's body as if stepping over a dead rodent and stopped a few paces from her. While one armoured hand held the handle of the great axe, the other hand removed the helmet. With a loud cracking of ice, the helmet came free and the lich dropped it into the water of the swamp with a splash.

"No. No." Katya was so horrified that she could barely squeak out even those simple words.

The face under the helmet was a twisted caricature of her own face, with brilliant yellow eyes shining like two tiny suns where her own grey-gold ones should be.

The lich-occupied Katya pointed at her, then spoke in a grating, creaking parody of her voice "You did this." The plate-mailed arm swept the clearing, taking in all the dead creatures therein. "You must also die. You no longer deserve your life."

The lich lifted the axe high overhead, then swung it towards the crying, unmoving Katya. It was all she could do to throw her arms up in a futile effort to block the heavy blade.

"Kat!"

The shaft of the axe struck her arms, and she resisted with all the strength she had left.

"Katya! Stop it! Wake up!"

Behind her, Fayne was squawking in panic. *At least she escaped*, Katya thought, relieved.

As the lich continued to push the blade downwards, Katya screamed, giving vent to her terror and pain and sadness.

"No!" Katya's scream as she woke up was incredibly loud in the confines of her bedroom.

"Kat! Please." The voice was hoarse.

Katya opened her eyes to see that her arm was across Lili's throat, cutting off her air supply, and that her lovely face was turning red under her tousled blonde hair.

Katya threw herself backwards to take the pressure off Lili's neck, rolling off the bed and landing crouched on the floor. She stood and crossed the room, quick as a cat, to light the lamp.

Lili was clutching the sheets around her shoulders. She bore two red marks, one on her face and one on her shoulder. Katya walked to the bed, unconcerned for her nakedness. In the weeks since she had first been intimate with Lili, she had gotten increasingly comfortable with letting herself show vulnerability around the human.

Katya sat on the edge of the bed. She wasn't sure if she should go to Lili or if she should leave her alone. Lili answered the question by holding out her arms.

Katya scurried over, laying her head down on the girl's blanket-covered legs. Lili draped one arm over Katya's bare shoulders and tangled her other hand in Katya's long red hair, a simple gesture Katya had quickly come to enjoy.

For a few minutes, neither of them spoke, Katya listening to Lili's breathing as it evened out again.

"Lili. I'm so sorry…it was…"

"It was a nightmare, Kat. I know. Maybe even more than that. I'm reading a book on sleep medicine right now that talks about something called night terrors. That's where a person thrashes around, sometimes even gets out of bed and moves around the room." She paused. "Or lashes out around them."

Katya rolled onto her back and looked closer at Lili's face. The red marks. Her eyes grew wide.

"Oh gods, Lili…did I hit you?"

"Yes." Lili knew there was no point in not being truthful. It was best for both of them. "You hit me twice. Not hard, not like I've seen you hit a training dummy, but enough to sting."

Katya's eyes filled with tears and her stomach lurched with the all-too familiar sinking that she always experienced when a nasty fight ended. The adrenaline built during her nightmare was leaving her body. The only evidence of her agitated sleep being Katya's slowing heart rate and the marks on the beautiful girl who had been sleeping beside her until a few minutes ago.

"I'm so sorry. I didn't know what was happening. You know I would never…"

"I know, Kat. Now be quiet and let me play with your hair some more."

Katya rolled her head back onto Lili's lap and shut her eyes, enjoying the feel of Lili's arm against her shoulder. Lili slid one foot from under the sheets and ran it up and down Katya's legs. Her foot was soft and warm, and the same clear lacquer from her fingernails adorned her toenails. Katya often teased her that her feet had obviously never seen the inside of boots that had trekked for years through all manner of hostile terrain. The extent of Katya's attention to her feet was that they needed to be dry and warm as much as possible. Pampering had never been a reality for her.

Fayne jumped down from her perch and fluttered to the bed. She walk-hopped over to where Lili's leg was tucked under the sheets and nestled against it. Settling in, she looked at the two women with clear affection.

After a few minutes of comfortable silence, Lili spoke. "Kat?"

"Yes?" Katya had almost fallen back asleep, but now opened her eyes and turned to face Lili.

"Kat...don't...don't you think it's time?"

"To get up?"

"No. Time to tell the whole story. To tell what happened before you left the swamp. There must be more. I've always wondered but never wanted to ask because it's something that has hurt you deeply. Maybe scarred is a better word."

Katya closed her eyes again, and sighed with resignation.

Lili pressed on. "Kat, if we're going to keep sharing a bed, which I very much enjoy, I need to know that I'm safe. That you're safe. I've been with you through three nightmares now, but this is the first time I've ever been scared. Whatever's causing you these horrible nights needs to come out of the dark place you've got it locked up in." She moved her fingers on Katya's shoulder, stroking the skin there. "When do you see Athena again?"

"Tomorrow. We had time together scheduled last week, but she got called away." Despite the sadness and fear surrounding her like a storm, Katya smiled at the memory of the letter Athena had left, written in her elegant green script.

Katya.

I'm sorry to have to do this with a note, but I had an urgent caller in the middle of the night who needed my help immediately. Of course, I can't talk about it, but if I recounted the situation, involving someone much like yourself who finds themselves at a crossroads, you would understand.

Please, let's keep this same day next week. Of course, if you really need me, come to the shop any time, but I always enjoy the long chats we have when the damn bell isn't ringing for someone who needs to buy dried flower petals or insect eyes.

From what I hear, you have someone keeping you company who is pleasant, attractive and insightful. I'm sure she's applying her own brand of healing, poking parts of your brain that you have forgotten existed. I approve.

See you next week. Warmest regards.

Athena.

The witch knew how to speak in a way that both reassured and built trust. Her manner was authoritative yet comforting all at once.

"Kat. Can you go today? Please? I'd say this is an emergency." She was near tears.

Without looking at her, Katya replied. "Yes. I'll go today. But I need you with me. I'm going to ask Jiris to be there, too. I owe all of you some answers, and the sooner everyone knows, the better it will be. I'll never heal the way I need to unless I tell the whole story to the people who want to help me get there."

Lili was silent for a moment before speaking. "Katya…are you sure? That is an incredible show of trust."

"Are you surprised?"

She wrinkled her face in thought before she answered. "I don't think the Katya I had dinner with that night at the square would have asked, but I'm not surprised that the Kat I've come to know is willing. You've already shared parts of your life, your other life, that I'm sure you never thought you would."

Katya reflected on this. She had shared war stories with the younger girl, yes, but for the first time had also talked about how she felt during those stories, the friends she mourned, the losses she learned from. About the Council of Oathtakers and what it meant to number among them. About her family, her identity, the relative uniqueness among elves about her relationships with other females.

And, after Lili had been sleeping next to her while she had a particularly vivid one, about her nightmares.

About anything and everything but the whole story of what had happened at the swamp.

"Kat?"

Lili's voice shook Katya from her reverie.

"I'm here. Just lost in thought."

"I can imagine." She paused before going on. "Are you sure you want me there? Because if you do, I'll go. I'll go because in my mind that means…well, it means that hopefully you want me in your future as well as your past. I've fallen in love with you, Katya, like I thought I would the day I first saw you."

Katya turned to look again at Lili, unsurprised at the girl's words. Her face, so beautiful even just out of sleep, held a hopefulness that verged on heart-breaking.

"I love you, Lili. I love you, and that's why I need you to hear what happened, because it might change how you feel and I can't bear the thought of you leaving, so if it's going to happen, I need it to happen now before I fall even deeper for you." Tears, once hated, were still rolling down her cheeks.

There was no hate in these tears, though...just hope.

Lili nodded, her own tears finally falling. She took Katya's hand, kissed it tenderly, and said, "I'm in this with you, Katya."

Katya wiped both her tears and Lili's, kissed the girl's hand in return then rolled off the bed in a backwards somersault and stood.

Lili smiled. "I never get tired of seeing that."

"Which? The somersault, or me naked?"

"Both are pretty amazing. You're very spry for a centenarian."

Katya smiled as she wrapped herself in a fur robe. "Impertinent young one." She crossed the room to the small desk and drew up two notes, then applied emerald green wax in the form of her bloodline crest leaf to seal them. She whistled to Fayne, who flew to her from where she had still been nuzzling into Lili's leg.

Katya presented her with the two notes, which she clamped in her beak. "One for Jiris, and the other for Athena. Wait while they reply, all right?"

Fayne squawked her understanding before Katya opened the window and the falcon flew off.

Lili was wide-eyed. "You're both still full of surprises. I had no idea she could do that."

"I told you, you're an impertinent youth who thinks she knows everything." Katya tossed another soft robe to Lili. "Let's have breakfast while we wait for her to come back."

Katya ordered food. By the time they were emptying the teapot, Fayne had returned. She passed the two reply notes she carried back to Katya.

Athena had written back in her green script.

Of course. See you at noon. A.

Jiris had written a simple response.

If I must, fine.

No surprise there.

She had her answers.

Once breakfast was cleared away, Katya indulged herself and Lili with a hot bath. The bathroom had a deep stone basin that drew both hot and cold water, and Katya had found, to her surprise, that she enjoyed soaking in a tub full of steaming water. Not only was it relaxing — and soothing to her many old aches and pains — she had found it was useful in helping her focus and collect her thoughts.

After drying off and watching Lili dress, Katya shooed her out of the room with a kiss. "I need some time to get ready."

Lili looked at her suspiciously. "Time to get ready to sit and talk? What do you need to do?"

Katya swallowed, nervous. "Combat meditation," she said in a low voice.

"Oh." Lili frowned. "It's that bad?

"Well, it's no battle, but I need to be focused. Meditation will help with that."

Lili reached out and took her hands. "Kat, remember. You won't be alone. You *aren't* alone."

Katya smiled. "Elias told me the same thing in my nightmare. It was the only good part."

"He sounds like a smart elf."

"He's his sister's brother. Now go. I'll see you in a few hours." She kissed Lili once more on the cheek as she closed the door.

From the other side, she heard, "Yes, ma'am."

She smiled. *Impertinent, indeed.*

Katya dropped her robe and sat on the bed cross-legged, enjoying the cool air on her naked skin after the bath. She closed her eyes and began breathing in an even, measured pace while tracing a repeating series of nine symbols in the air.

She had been taught this form of meditation by an assassin called the Smiling Lioness. Katya had never learned her real name, which was fine with her. She had been looking for education, not friendship. It had cost the elf a brutal one-on-one duel that she had to win to learn her secrets, and they had opposing viewpoints on the moralities of assassination, but that aside, they had been able to teach each other valuable skills.

After nine cycles of nine symbols, Katya had settled deep into meditation. She stayed in that state, pondering the many possibilities the day held, until Fayne chirped, bringing her out of her contemplative state.

"Time to get ready, huh? Thank you, love."

She climbed off the bed and dressed. She was very close to wearing her armour and weapons. It seemed symbolic of the struggle she felt she was about to face, but on reflection, she decided against it. She needed to tackle what was coming with friends, not arms and armour.

A few minutes later, both the elf and her bird were heading into the bright sunlight of Fandalore, towards the only encounter that Katya had ever been terrified of before it began.

Chapter Ten

Eight months after Day Zero

"Thank you all for being here. I know this isn't the usual arrangement this office sees." Katya was trying to give the impression that she was relaxed by making some small talk before the inevitable storm began, an immense difference from the surly silence she had displayed upon her first meeting with Athena.

Elf, bird, witch, greyling and human were all sitting in Athena's library, where she and Katya had spent so many hours, time that had been building inevitably to this moment. The witch had worked her magic, transforming a room that was normally just big enough for two chairs to include three more seats, a perch for Fayne and a table holding an assortment of beverages.

Athena answered first. "It may be unusual, yes, but the whole point of these discussions is your comfort and your healing. If having us here will help, that's fine."

Katya nodded. "Thank you. I..." Her voice faltered for a moment. "I need the support. I can't do this alone."

Saying that out loud felt so strange. She was someone who had always been ready to plunge headlong into the next fight, numbers be damned.

Jiris spoke, gesturing at her with his pipe as he did. "You're a far cry from the elf who stormed out of my clinic a week after showing up with infection and heat stroke and insisted on heading right back into the fray."

"Jiris, really. Must you smoke that foul thing in here? I just had the draperies cleaned." Athena gestured at the pipe, which stopped smoking.

"Fine," the old healer grumped. "I'll sit here like a lump and chew on the damn thing."

"That would be a pleasant change. Katya, please, go on."

Before proceeding, Katya poured two glasses of the light green nectar that Athena kept a sizeable supply of, handing one to Lili before sipping from her own, gathering her thoughts.

"I've told each of you different things since getting here. Jiris knows the story of what brought me to him and some of what has happened during my ups and downs here. Athena has heard those things and more, and got me answering questions I didn't want to face but knew I would have to if I was ever going to move on."

She faced Lili. "And you've heard more about me than almost anyone else in my life."

Katya took another swallow of her drink. "I thank each of you for what you've done, for how you've healed me in one way or another." Her small audience either nodded or smiled.

"But there's a part of the tale of that day in the swamp that I haven't told any of you. It's a horrible story, and one that I take no pride in. When I tell you, you'll understand why."

Katya sighed, made herself as comfortable as possible, and took a deep breath.

"So, up to what you all know, about everyone in the party being killed by the brain scarab exploding, is true. The tale of fighting the lich is true. The rest of the story…what happened in between…well, that starts after I went to Shira's side…"

* * * *

Day Zero

"Katya." Shira's gloved hand found hers. "You were my finest student. You long ago surpassed me as a warrior." He paused to take a breath, an act that clearly caused him immense pain. "But you were also like my daughter, and I have always thanked the gods that I had that experience."

His body was racked with a series of coughs. After he quieted again, he continued.

"So let me talk like a father before I die. You have to learn the last lesson we talked about. Patience. Restraint. Control. Your skills are finer than any warrior I've ever crossed swords with, but you've always been impetuous and overeager. Please promise me…you'll learn when it's time to fight, and when it's time to…"

"To walk away." Tears, hated tears, were now flowing. Distantly, Katya could hear Fayne on her shoulder, cooing to calm her.

"I promise."

Shira squeezed her hand and opened his eyes one last time. "Thank you. If you mean that, then you've learned my last lesson. Goodbye, Katya."

His eyes closed and life left his body. She continued to hold his hand, hesitant to let it go, not wanting to break the last connection with the man who had been closer to her than anyone in the world. She had spent more time with Shira than anybody else in her life, first as his student, then as a fellow Oathtaker.

As an elf, she would ultimately have outlived him. But it shouldn't have happened yet.

There was so much they had planned to do.

They had never visited the pirate-ridden waters of the Bottomless Gulf. Never explored the Temple of the Black Geyser, rumoured to be full of massive bats that could carry off a human. Never sampled twenty-year-old Angel's Whisky from the legendary Purple Jaguar Inn.

Their days of sparring, trading blow for blow and walking away with the best of each other's skills, were over.

They would never again argue around a massive campfire about magic or the best material for shield-making or a province's politics.

Nothing.

Rage, white-hot, was building within her.

Completely lost, Katya had no idea how to give vent to her rage, despite years of carrying herself like she always knew what needed to be done next.

For a long time, she knelt in the cold mist of the swamp, watching the body of her mentor. When the chill became too much, she either had to take some action or die in the swamp like those lying scattered around the clearing.

"Oh, but you do know what to do," said the voice in her mind. *"You know exactly what to do. There's a whole camp full of revenge just a walk away."*

"But I promised Shira…" This she said out loud, cutting the flat silence of the cold air.

"Walk away after you avenge his death. That's what you do. You kill. And you do it better than anyone else." The voice in her head was growing more insistent and making more sense.

Fayne's chirping brought her back. The bird recognised that Katya was waging some internal battle. Katya listened as Fayne questioned her.

"Bury them, I guess. Or lay them in the swamp. The water and mud at the bottom will preserve them. Lay them with their weapons, take anything usable. That's the pact we all made."

Fayne spoke again. Even as she did, Katya found herself turning away, facing the enemy camp sitting across the swamp and the vengeance that waited there.

When the falcon saw this, Fayne's vocalising took on a higher pitch.

"I know what I said, and I know we should walk away. But I owe the lizards for what they did. Look around, Fayne. They think we're all dead. I *should* be dead. I can take them by surprise."

The bird twittered at her with a note of reproach in her song, telling Katya that she was letting hatred and rage cloud her judgement.

Katya replied without looking at the bird, still staring into the fog. "Fine, you don't have to go. Stay here with Shira."

Fayne tried once more, sadness now creeping into her song.

"I'll be back." She tapped the perch on her shoulder and Fayne flew to her. Katya gently stroked her feathers. "Please, love...just wait for me. You don't need to be there. Now go sit with Shira. We can start honouring him that way."

With a soft chirp, Fayne left her perch and settled on Shira's armoured shoulder. She ruffled her feathers once, then began a quiet, cooing song of mourning.

Fighting back more tears, Katya set off into the swamp.

* * * *

Eight months after Day Zero

"So, Shira asked you to make a promise." A statement from Athena, not a question.

"Yes. A promise to learn the thing he had tried to teach me over and over. The same thing Jiris did his best to remind me of the day that I fought the lich. The same thing other people have tried and failed to show me. That sometimes there really is black and white...not just grey. That the best way isn't always head-on into danger. That's the whole reason I spent time training like an assassin, even though I don't like killing from the shadows, because sometimes the quieter, less chaotic path is the best one."

"So...why do you think, Kat, that you usually choose...chose that chaotic path?" Lili's dark blue eyes were full of sadness when she looked at the elf.

Katya glanced around the room before she answered, seeking support. She found it when she locked eyes with Fayne, who chirped encouragement. She understood what Katya was trying to say.

"I chose that path because I could do it so damn well. Shira always told me if he could have created a machine that was built for combat, he would have used me as the blueprint. The perfect warrior, he called me. He spent years forging these skills in me, sharpened them, told me about the Council and how I could use those skills for good, and then..." She stopped.

"Then what?" asked Athena.

"Then used me! I never saw that until now. I loved him like a parent, but he used me. So has the Council." Her voice was controlled but full of anger.

How odd it sounded to say it out loud.

"He convinced me that taking the Blood Oath was the best way to apply my skills and I was so enthralled with myself as a warrior that I believed him. I became a weapon."

The room was quiet. Katya looked at Lili to see her eyes brimming with tears.

Katya spoke again, the anger rising. "And it's not fair. As he got older, he started trying to teach me restraint and patience while always telling me what a gifted warrior I was. It's not fair that he did that to me, made me what and who I am now, and then started trying to convince me that I shouldn't use what he taught me. What he brought out in me. I felt like I was being torn in two sometimes."

She closed her eyes before continuing.

"That's why I always chose that path of chaos—because somewhere, deep in the back of my mind, I knew it wasn't fair to ask me to use restraint when everything I had learned was designed to push me forward. Fighting was an easy path."

She paused and took a breath. "He and the Council wanted a tool that they could use when needed to accomplish a mission but could just put away when it wasn't time to kill anymore. Maybe when he started urging me to always think twice about swinging a sword, he was trying to soothe his own conscience about all the death he had seen himself. Or maybe he felt guilty for what he had done to me. I don't know." She downed a large swallow of her drink, but she couldn't hide the shaking of her hand.

"His dying wish was for me to make a promise that he must have known I could never keep. I feel like he took my life out of my hands when he convinced me to swear my Oath. Then he made me promise I wouldn't do what the Oath obligated me to do so he could find peace before he died."

Her voice was starting to tremble with emotion. "He found peace. I found torment. It hurt then. It hurts more now after months of thinking about it all. I'm not sure if I'll ever know again what it is I'm supposed to do. I feel like I've lost my life." Overwhelmed by emotion, Katya buried her face in her hands and began to sob.

The room sat silent around her. After a few minutes, from between her fingers, Katya spoke again, her voice just above a whisper. "If I can't be that weapon any more, that machine, then what am I?"

Katya's words had also brought Lili to tears, despite the immense differences in their ages and life experience.

Athena took advantage of the silence to calm the emotional storm that Katya had put herself through. "Katya, my dear, you are, to use an old healer's expression, deeply in the reeds. But you're not alone. While you may have lost one group of warriors, it appears to me that in this room you've created new bonds that will help you keep moving on."

After a few minutes, Katya rubbed her eyes with the palms of her hand and sat up straight.

"Katya. Can you look at me?" Athena's voice was quiet.

The elf met her gaze with red and puffy eyes.

"Shira was an old warrior. You know better than anyone how many battles, both real and inside his head, he fought during his lifetime. Rangers of his vintage never shared their ghosts, their demons. He had countless things he was grappling with. I would guess he taught you that you don't talk about those things you saw when you closed your eyes or that woke you up screaming."

Athena sipped from her green drink before speaking again. "The usual thoughts about war have always been that as long as a soldier could swing a sword, they could fight. I'm not saying that's any excuse for what either of you did or didn't do or for what happened between you, but I want you to understand the state his thoughts were in when he died.

"Regardless of what he made of you and your skills, I have no doubt he did indeed see you not just as a comrade, but as a daughter. He sacrificed his own life to save you — if he hadn't taken those few seconds to push you underwater, he could have ducked himself and his armour would have kept him alive."

"That's true," Katya said. Her voice was muffled through the hands she had placed over her face once more.

"He had to know that he took you into a life that would change you forever. He taught you many things, but never prepared you for what you would see, hear, taste, smell and remember as you wandered the world."

Athena took a moment to smooth her robes. "I, too, wonder if the lessons about using that quieter path he kept trying to teach you in the time before he died were his way of making up for that. I'm sure he saw you changing, becoming…darker, shall we say, long before your final battle together. Maybe that was his last effort to bring you back to some version of the elf he first met."

Silence again descended on the room.

"Kat?" Despite the emotion on her face, the Lili's voice was steady.

She looked at Lili. "Yes?"

"Do you feel guilty for surviving?"

Katya tilted her head, curious. "What do you mean?"

"Do you feel like you should have died as well? A noble death? A warrior's death?"

Katya had thought about this a few times. Briefly, but she had indeed thought about it. "No. No, I don't feel that. Fortunes of war are what they are. If we were standing in different spots, it might have been me pushing Shira into the water. We all did what we were trained to do. The gods rolled the dice and the game went on."

Athena perked up at that comment. "Katya, you said you all did what you were trained to do."

"Yes."

"So, would you say you all responded as you should have?"

"Yes. Everyone played their role in the fight as I expected. I trusted them to do that. We were a team. We knew what each other would do." Katya frowned. *Where is the witch going with this now?*

"Had any of you ever dealt with a brain scarab before?"

"I'm…not sure. Probably just Shira, I would guess. I didn't have a chance to ask anyone else." She said this with bitterness and regret.

"So, it was an…unusual encounter, then? One out of your realm of experience?"

"You could say that, yes."

Athena leaned forward, tapping her fingertips together. "So, is it fair to say that you had a normal response to an abnormal situation?"

What the hell?

"I suppose you could say that, too."

"Excellent." Athena sat back. "You just defined the injury to your mind. An expected response to a highly unusual occurrence. Everything you've told us so far fits."

She started ticking items off on her fingers. "You did what you were trained to do when faced with a new and different enemy, the brain scarab. You tried to honour your dead comrades in the customary way, even though you knew you weren't in full health and that it would take you back to a place that would create strong emotions in you. When confronted with the remains of Shira's body, you reacted with fear, dread and horror, all understandable. But you still let your Oath and your training guide you." She paused for a moment, eyes closed, further collecting her thoughts.

"In other words, you have consistently acted in your normal fashion when confronted with strange, even terrifying, situations. The many different moods and reactions you've had over these last few months are your body and brain trying to protect you from echoes of those things. Feeling on edge. Trying to escape your memories through drinking. Fighting your impulses to stay away from harm. Going back to the swamp. Fighting at the tavern."

Athena leaned back. "Basically, my dear, the thoughts and feelings that make you hide in waiting or rush in swinging have been like a shield, to use an analogy you can envision, trying to protect you. But you haven't let that happen. You've been battling your own brain and body. If you accept that, you can start to tame these things that have been spinning you in circles."

Katya stared at her, dumbfounded. The witch had summed up her last few months in two minutes. Her words, her logic, were starting to illuminate things in Katya's mind she had previously ignored.

She sat back in her chair, taking this all in.

"Is that when you left the swamp, girl?" Jiris asked her. "What got you onto the road to town?"

Katya sat back up, her stomach twisting. With all the emotional turmoil of the last few revelatory minutes, she had forgotten that she still had to tell the story of the encampment.

"No. No, there's more." She closed her eyes. "And, please. Please listen, because right now I only have the strength to tell it one time."

She didn't open her eyes when she began speaking again. It seemed easier that way. "Despite what I had promised, I made my way to the lizard man camp on the other side of the swamp. I had directions from Fayne, so it wasn't difficult to find my way…"

* * * *

Afternoon of Day Zero

Katya opened her eyes into a setting sun with no immediate idea how long she had been unconscious or how she had gotten that way. She groaned as she sat up. Her arms and shoulders ached from exertion, there was a deep throbbing pain in her side and her leg was covered in dried blood. Her back was against a firm surface.

The sunlight was coming through a doorway. She was inside a small structure, sitting directly across from the open door, with the rear wall of the building to her back.

Before she figured out the circumstances that got her there, she needed to do a quick check to see where and how she was injured. She pushed herself up the wall using her legs until she was standing. Shaky, but standing.

Moving deepened the pain in her side. Sliding her hand down her torso, Katya encountered ragged edges of torn leather armour and a deep wound beneath it. She moved to the sharper pain in her left leg and discovered an arrow broken off, the head still lodged in her thigh. Luckily, it wasn't deep and with some time she'd be able to work it out of her flesh. She was grateful that it wasn't poisoned.

She ran her hands over the rest of her body, finding nicks and cuts in her armour, but no other injuries aside from the one in her shoulder the lizard man chieftain had caused during the first battle.

She moved on to a weapons check. She reached over her shoulder to check Isshogai and the Last Whisper. Both were mounted where they should be, but the act of stretching deepened the intense ache in her arms and shoulders. The pain moved through to her back and chest. Whatever had happened, she had exerted herself immensely.

She removed both weapons and inspected them. They had seen heavy use, although the sword was already repairing the wear it had undergone. Even in the dimming sunlight, the decorative plates on the crossbow were warped, almost melted. Something had applied immense heat to the metal, but Katya had no idea what.

The sword was covered with sticky brown blood.

Lizard man blood.

The fog over her brain was beginning to thin, much like the mist fading away after the earlier battle in the swamp.

The swamp. Her friends. Shira's death. A long walk. Explosions. Fire.

Things began rushing back to her, images and smells and sounds of combat. A frenzied trek through the swamp to the lizard camp. Three sentries she had killed with the crossbow while hiding among the trees. The look on the face of the first lizard man she had stabbed through the heart when she vaulted over the perimeter fence.

What the hell did I do?

After a rushed inventory of the rest of her weapons — expandable staff intact, axinite dagger broken, both throwing knives and her shorter sword missing — she painfully made her way to the door. The smell of smoke hit her before leaving the hut.

When she stepped outside, she remembered everything in one horrible, nauseating wave.

The remains of what had been the lizard camp smouldered around her. Tents, clothing, the rough fence of sharpened trees...anything that could burn was either destroyed or still smoking. Somehow, the small shed where she had awoken had been spared, but barely — flames were starting to lick at a pile of firewood next to the shed and would have spread the fire to her refuge. She walked over to the firewood and gingerly kicked the smoking pieces off the pile so they wouldn't ignite the rest.

Scattered among the smoky ruins of the camp were bodies.

Katya saw piles of dead lizard men in various states of damage. Some had limbs cut clean away from their body, and some had been beheaded. One had been pinned to a large tree with Katya's shorter sword. Several had multiple shots from her crossbow evident on their chests.

To her left, she spotted one of her throwing knives, buried to the hilt in a lizard skull. A couple bodies had no visible wounds at all. However, their heads lay at unnatural angles. Their necks had been snapped.

To her mounting shock, she realised that some of the bodies were shorter and thinner in stature and decorated with swirls of what looked like berry juice.

Females. Not warriors, but caretakers.

She spun around the rest of the clearing...more females, and in a few spots, very small versions of the lizard folk.

Children. By the gods, I killed children.

In one far corner of the camp, there was a cluster of crumpled bodies. She moved closer but stopped in horror as soon as she could see what had happened. A lizard man holding an axe lay on the ground, his chest sliced open. Behind him was a female, her back to the clearing, two dead young ones in her arms. All three of them had been killed with crossbow bolts.

All she could do was close her eyes for a few moments.

Had she done all this? In her rage and pain and thirst for revenge, had she destroyed the whole camp?

She needed to know everything. She methodically made her way through the camp, accompanied by the sound of sputtering flames and the smell of burnt wood and flesh, and counted the dead. Twenty-two, not including the three sentries she had killed before she had arrived at the camp proper.

After she finished her inspection of the camp, checked each body for signs of life and how it had died, Katya came to the inevitable conclusion. She had done this all by herself.

There had been no mystery allies, no members of her party that had miraculously survived, no reinforcements from a nearby settlement. With the weapons at her disposal, and in some cases her bare hands, she had caused this carnage. No wonder all the muscles in her upper body ached.

But she hadn't taken her revenge out on the lizard warriors they had been asked to drive off. She had lost her senses and slaughtered all of them, regardless of gender or age or complicity with robbing caravans and killing merchants.

She dropped to her knees. Even after decades of confronting death, the enormity of what she had done, especially considering her promise to Shira as he lay dying, sickened her. She vomited what little food she had eaten that day, her stomach hitching until it was empty. She wiped her mouth with the back of her hand

and rose to her feet on legs that felt like they were made of rope.

For the second time that day, she stood completely lost. Spying a water skin, she limped over to it, praying it was full. It was, and she drank deeply from it, grateful for the cool liquid sliding down her throat.

Her hands were trembling.

She could no longer ignore the rising lump in her throat.

Katya threw her head back and screamed with rage and fury and grief. Louder and longer than she could have imagined, she vented the events of the last twelve hours, not caring if it attracted more enemies, not caring if she lived or died at that moment.

It was a scream that made the tamer animals of the forest scurry for their homes, a scream that caused predators who had smelled death in the air and were coming towards the camp for an easy meal to turn around. Predators knew danger when they heard it, and that scream was from a creature far more dangerous than themselves.

Lengths away, Fayne, still perched on Shira's shoulder, awoke from a light sleep. Her sensitive ears heard Katya scream and it set her heart to racing. She took to the sky, racing for the camp.

At the camp, Katya stood in the silence left in the wake of her emotional venting. Her mind was flooded with images of battles and deaths past and present, some of them seeming so real she felt she was reliving them.

She fell again to her knees, ignoring the pain across her body. The wound in her side began bleeding. She didn't care. The arrowhead in her leg throbbed. She reached down and pulled the arrow out, the barbs tearing her skin, screaming in pain as she did so. She tossed the arrow away and let that wound bleed as well.

She curled up on her unhurt side, eyes closed, all pretence of being a warrior gone. Right now she was just a young elf whose skill, tools and confidence meant nothing.

That morning, Katya had been part of a family of Oath-bound warriors fighting the worst creatures the world had to offer. Now, hours later, she was badly wounded. Exhausted. Uncertain. Lying in the dirt surrounded by a score of corpses she created. She had killed innocents, guilty of nothing aside from being part of their race and in the wrong place at the wrong time.

A sudden rustle of feathers appeared in front of her. Katya opened her eyes to see Fayne settling to the ground. Her dark eyes were tinged with sadness. The bird chirped a few notes.

"Yes. It was me. All me."

Fayne looked around at the carnage her mistress had caused. The bodies. The fires. The death.

Giving a bird's version of a sigh, Fayne hopped across the ground to where Katya lay, her head resting on one outstretched arm. Fayne hopped to the crook of Katya's neck and snuggled in.

Katya, with some effort, lifted her other arm and moved it to where she could stroke Fayne's feathers. The bird chirped and fell asleep. Apparently, regardless of Fayne's thoughts about what Katya had done, she was forgiven.

With this act of love, Katya gave in to the tears she had held back since waking up in the hut.

She wept for her lost friends and mentor. For the lizard men and families she had so brutally killed just for being themselves and for trying to survive. Killing a raiding party was one thing—wiping out an entire encampment who would have left anyways was quite another.

And she wept for herself.

She cried until she had no more tears. Too exhausted to even move inside, she closed her eyes and asked the gods above for protection as she faded into sleep.

Bird and elf lay together, two exhausted warriors, until the hazy sunrise of the next day.

Chapter Eleven

Day One

Katya opened her eyes to the dim light of dawn. She tried her best to sit up, but failed, only making it halfway up. Her body was still racked with pain, even after a long night's sleep. She lay back down, took a deep breath then sat up at a slower pace. Fayne, who had taken to the air as soon as Katya stirred, was sitting on what had been a support post for the perimeter fence.

Overnight, the fires had burned out, leaving only blackened timbers and stumps. The dead lizard men were lying in the same spots they had been when Katya had dropped into unconsciousness. Some of them had been picked at by night scavengers. Remarkably, nothing had bothered her or Fayne.

Katya felt horrible. Her mouth was once again dry and tasted of ashes, her stomach rumbled with hunger and every muscle in her body still ached. Her wounds were hot and she could feel her pulse beating in the injured areas — strong signs of infection.

She wrinkled her nose at the smell of stale sweat and dried blood and mud on her body. Fayne, with her keen sense of smell, must have been overwhelmed by the odour. She did, in fact, look a bit put out.

Despite the circumstances, Katya laughed. "Sorry."

Fayne's reply was a reminder about the importance of good grooming.

"I've been a bit busy. But I don't blame you if you want to stay away from me until I can find some water."

Katya recalled a clear stream outside the encampment, in the direction of where the first battle with the lizards had taken place. Back where her friends had died. Back where Shira, who had saved her life, lay lifeless and cold. The image of his face floated in front of her eyes.

She shook her head, dismissing the image. This was not the time for being sentimental or for further giving in to emotions. It was time to do what she did best, which was to survive.

She turned to Fayne. "Hey, be a good bird and see if you can find a stream about two lengths back that way. I need a drink and a bath."

Squawking in agreement with the bath comment, Fayne took off.

Looking around the burned-out camp, Katya forced herself to ignore the bodies and seek out usable supplies — food, medicine, water, weapons. She decided not to take any valuables she came across. She had dishonoured this village enough.

In the back of the small hut where she had sheltered, she found sacks of dried meat and some small, wrinkled fruit. She nibbled the fruit, hoping that something a lizard man's gut could withstand wouldn't kill her. The small bite she took was sweet. No numbness on her tongue or lips, no bitterness, no burning. *Hopefully that means no poison.*

After a few minutes, she took a larger bite and swallowed. The fruit tasted wonderful and caused no ill effects even after sitting in her stomach for a bit. She ate two pieces of the fruit, followed by two strips of the dried meat. She tried not to think about what the meat might be from, but it was salty and fortifying. She packed an empty sack full of both foods.

She left the shed, hoping to find some medicine, but nothing else usable was left. She retrieved her throwing daggers but left her sword where it was, pinning the lizard man to the tree. In her mind she could feel the resistance the blade would present to her hand, could hear the sucking noise it would make when she pulled it loose. The thought sickened her.

She made her way out of the encampment and walked towards the stream, favouring her right side and limping on her damaged left leg. The deep gash in her side, caused by a bladed weapon of some kind, had stopped bleeding overnight but still ached. The punctures in her leg and shoulder dribbled blood.

After a few minutes, Fayne returned, confirming for her that she was on track for the stream. A half hour's walk brought her to the rushing water. She wasn't relishing a dip into what was sure to be an icy bath, especially since a cold mist was once again hanging in the air.

Katya stripped off her armour, noting the spots where it was damaged and would need repair. After a few moments of hesitation, she stripped off her boots and bodysuit as well, and removed the now useless medicine poultice she had put on her shoulder the day before. *In for an emerald, in for the crown.*

The soft ground of the swamp was cold and oozed in an unpleasant fashion under her bare feet. It was a small relief to get to the more solid rocks of the streambank. She spent a few minutes square breathing, preparing herself for the cold.

When she was ready, she waded into the stream. Even with preparation, it was incredibly frigid, and when the water washed over the wounds in her leg and side, she gasped in a mix of shock and relief.

Still, elves were nothing if not hearty, and before long, Katya was comfortable enough to sink into the water up to her shoulders. She ran her hands over her skin, washing away the grime of the last day, and gently probed her wounds, letting the cold rush of water cleanse them. Looking down, she saw that the blood streaming away in the current was bright red, not the darker crimson that would have marked the wounds as infected.

Putting her face underwater, she drank deep from the stream, the cold water down her parched throat a blessing. She could hold her breath for several minutes, so she took the time to also loosen her hair. Facing into the current, she let the water streel her hair out behind her. It had been ages since her hair had not been bound up, and for a minute, she remembered what regular elven girls lived with all the time. In her life, though, long hair trailing down her back was something an enemy could grab on to.

"Your old life, you mean." Lovely. The voice in her head had woken up.

She closed her eyes, willing the cold water to push the inside voice away. This was not the time to be considering decisions about anything other than her immediate future.

Katya stayed underwater until her lungs began to ache, then stood, popping her head and shoulders out of the water to scan the area. All clear.

Her hair hung down her neck like a cold scarf, and she was surprised at how good it felt to have clean hair.

She waded out of the stream, refreshed both inside and out. She looked down at the cuts and punctures on her body. All were leaking blood. To her surprise, the sight made tears well up again.

Angry, she squeezed her eyes shut. She had seen herself wounded many times. It was a hazard of her calling. Why this reaction today? The memory of how and where the wounds happened? Shock at the events of the last two days?

She didn't know and it didn't matter. Like her future, complex emotions could be sorted out after survival.

She picked up her bodysuit and walked back into the stream, letting the current run through the suit. The material had almost completed repairing itself where it had been cut through the armour. However, despite the enchantment to keep the suit clean and in good repair, dirt still rinsed out of the suit when she submerged it. When the stream ran clear through the suit, she climbed out of the water and wrung the fabric out until it was almost dry. It was still damp when she put it back on, but at least it was now some protection against the cold, mist-filled air. Not to mention well-cleaned for the first time in months.

Fayne, keeping watch from a nearby tree, clucked her approval.

After emptying out the various pockets and pouches built into her armour, Katya took each piece to the water's edge, scrubbing the leather with a piece of light volcanic rock she used to clean the tough material. There was a darker bloodstain around the cut in the armour's side that would need cleaning solvent to remove, but she did the best she could under the circumstances.

She did the same with her boots, belt, weapon bandoliers and, lastly, her weapons.

Before cleaning her crossbow, she examined the decorative etchings on the stock more carefully. The metal was bowed outward as well as melted. The heat that had damaged the metal had come from within the crossbow itself.

Gods above, how many times did I fire it?

She had obviously put a tremendous amount of energy through the weapon when she had been using it. She put it aside, hoping that a mechanist could repair it. She would hate to lose such a valuable tool.

"But maybe it would serve you right," her inner voice prompted. She ignored it.

While her equipment dried, Katya looked around the small clearing where she had bathed. She had a good knowledge of medicinal plants—she was no witch but knew enough to get by. Spotting some thin yellow moss on the bank of the stream, she smiled in satisfaction.

She cut three squares of the moss, which had a mild numbing effect when placed against the skin and was highly absorbent. Reaching under the bodysuit, she placed a square against each of the wounds she had, closing her eyes in relief as the moss went to work, killing the pain and stopping the blood flow. Her suit was snug enough that the fabric would keep the moss in place. It wasn't ideal but it would do until she could find a proper healer.

Finally, her armour and weapons were serviceable, her wounds were patched and her hunger and thirst were sated. She tapped her shoulder, and Fayne settled on her perch.

Katya looked in the direction of the bodies of her friends and mentor. They were owed a proper burial, and they carried many valuables and supplies that Katya could use. She agonised—she was obligated to return to the site of the battle and explosion, but she weighed that against the fact that she was a wounded and under-equipped elf at this point.

She decided that, no matter how much it went against everything she felt, until she was rested and healed, she couldn't properly take care of her comrades. She would find a town, one with a healer and an armourer who could repair her damaged chest plate and a weapon shop where she could replace her axinite dagger and get the crossbow looked at.

Yes, a sound, logical plan—she needed to rely on some logic after being pushed by nothing but emotion for the last day. When she was patched up and re-supplied, she would return and honour her dead.

"Really? Is that really what's going on?" The voice in her head was speaking again. *"Or are you afraid to see what's there? The bodies. A battle that you survived when the others didn't."*

"No," Katya whispered aloud. "That's not it. Fortunes of war."

"Tell yourself that. Think you can live with the fact that you survived, and that Shira died to save you?"

"If he hadn't, we all would have died. He went out the way he wanted — as a warrior, sacrificing himself. He helped me survive to tell the story and honour their memory." She had again spoken out loud, this time with more force.

Fayne cocked her head at Katya's speech, seeming confused by the elf speaking to no one.

"If Shira hadn't spent his last seconds saving you, he could have turned away from the scarab. He would be alive, like he should be, and you would be dead, like you deserve."

"No!" This time, it was a shout. "Fate played out. He died, I lived. I honour his memory and the memory of the rest who fell. Be silent."

The voice laughed. *"You honour his memory by going against his last wish and killing a pack of innocent lizard folk?"*

Katya had no reply.

The voice shrugged. *"I thought so. Time will tell what happens, won't it, girl?"* With this, the voice faded away.

For a few moments, Katya stared into the rushing water of the stream. A curious chirp from Fayne brought her back to reality.

"No, I'm fine."

Fayne gave another chirp.

"Yes, really. Now why don't you do what you do and go find us a town to hole up in for a few days?"

With a cry of joy, Fayne launched herself into the air, happy to be away from where they had been, that place of cold and death.

Katya watched her falcon sail upwards. When Fayne was nothing more than a speck in the sky, she began walking with the flow of water. Shira had taught her, when in doubt, always walk downstream. At some point, she would find a grain grinder or sawmill using the stream to function. Civilisation was what she could find in a pinch and right now she needed some civilisation.

His face floated in front of her again.

She would miss him.

* * * *

Eight months after Day Zero

"And that's when we found the road, then the town, then all of you." Katya looked around the room. Fayne and Jiris stared at her with sad eyes.

Lili was still crying, but looked thoughtful. "It's kind of ironic, Kat. The day I was able to hold your sword, when you showed me some movement with it. I remember wondering about its name, and how it seemed odd. It's called 'for life' but you use it to kill in the name of the Council. Is that good? Is protecting one life worth taking another? Is it you killing or the sword?" She took a drink from her glass, like speaking even those few words had parched her throat. "Your story makes all those things I thought about…more real, I guess. It's no wonder you have been struggling — you carry so much in your mind."

Only Athena's expression was unreadable. She spoke. "Katya. How do you feel now, having told that story?"

"Better, I suppose. Like a secret that was dragging me down is gone. But guilty. Ashamed."

"Guilt and shame are different, yes, but I can see why you would be experiencing both. What I can't imagine, what none of us will ever be able to imagine, is what you experienced when you attacked the camp. We have no ability to judge, nor should we. None of us have ever been, or ever will be, in that position. It must have been a remarkable mental and physical strain on you."

She paused to adjust how she sat. "Do you feel guilty for killing those lizard men?"

"Yes."

"Why?"

"They had no reason to die. We were never even supposed to go near their camp. The idea was to take out a small raiding party as a warning to stop destroying trade caravans. Before the brain scarab came roaring out of the trees at us, I was ready to tackle the whole camp no matter what. Shira had talked me out of it, but I felt we should take the camp." She thought for a moment. "At least, I thought we had to wipe them out."

"Because they were evil?"

"Yes. That was my thinking." Katya managed a partial smile. "But this girl I know has engaged me in some excellent discussions lately about how evil is subjective."

"She sounds like a very intelligent girl. Now, you were saying…?"

Katya swallowed some of her own drink. Her mouth and throat were dry. "It wasn't even that they were lizard men. They could have been slavers or pirates or some kind of undead. We were asked to put a stop to them and as usual, I wanted to rush headlong into a fight even though it wasn't needed. Shira made the right choice by saying we should leave."

"And then you made the opposite choice when it came to the camp later that day." It wasn't a question.

"Yes."

"Even though you had promised Shira that you would heed his lesson of walking away when it was the right time to do so?"

"Yes." It was a whisper.

"Would you do it again now? Attack the encampment?"

"No. I'd killed before, but never like that. Not just attacking anyone in my way. I'll live with the guilt of that. But if I could relive that day, I would do what Shira wanted, mourn and bury my comrades, and never go back."

Athena smiled. "Well, that's progress then, isn't it?" She took a moment to smooth her robes before speaking again.

"Katya. You have been very hard on yourself. I don't believe you've been right to do so, but I understand why you have. Your feelings about all this won't change overnight, and it will take continued healing."

She took a moment to refill her glass. "In the meantime, though, I want you to think about a few things.

"You never did have a chance to mourn your friends. The day they died, you...lost your senses, let's say, and were forced into a situation where you had to leave them behind so you would survive. When you went back, everything you planned was thrown into chaos by your encounter with the lich."

Katya nodded. "Yes."

"You were with Shira when he died. You sent him to the next life, whatever it might be, and honoured him as you thought best. You did the same for him a second time when you shrouded his body. Your feelings about him and how he shaped your life, even after he died, are not simple, and something that we'll have to discuss at some length, I think. I would daresay there will be some issues with your parents mixed in there as well. After all, he became a surrogate father to you, don't you think?"

Katya thought of her mother, who loved her but didn't really understand Katya's life or the toll it had taken on her. Like Lili's mother, her mother wanted to be a grandmother and wasn't shy about saying so.

"True, yes."

"I think you *do* have some aspect of survivor's guilt. Most warriors do, at least the ones who live long enough to become old. You said that you felt guilty for what happened at the camp, but not for being the only one who made it out alive. But you also said that the next morning at the stream you had an imaginary war of words with yourself about whether you should have lived, troubling you enough that Fayne noticed. That's something we also need to talk about more."

At hearing her name, Fayne chirped, reminding everyone that, in her opinion, she had been right all along. That raised a smile from all, save for Jiris, who called her a "damn talking feather duster."

"Finally, you have to look at your sense of identity. Your spirit. Who you are without your armour. I'm glad to see that this is something you appear to have already been exploring, both alone and with help." Athena glanced at Lili, who, while no longer crying, clearly understood the immensity of the issues facing the elf she had allowed into her life.

"How you look at right and wrong, how you see good and evil, has been mixed with being an Oathtaker for so long that you've lost your balance about those things. That's the shame you mentioned. You're questioning everything you thought you knew."

She paused for a moment, lost in thought. "You said you see yourself as a weapon, a tool...yes?"

"I do." The elf's voice was bitter, almost contemptuous.

"I'd like you to reconsider that. With exceptions, a weapon or a tool has no mind of its own. Your own sword, for example, seems to have some form of awareness. But most of them are simply held in the hand or pointed at an enemy and used. A regular knife or a club has no intent, no compassion, no discretion."

Athena leaned forward in her chair.

"But you do have those things, Katya. Think about what you've done since you've been here. Entertaining the children in the fountain square with Fayne. Dealing with that brute Alog without killing him. Training groups of girls, showing them that they can become anything and everything they want and that a girl can be the equal of any boy."

Katya's eyes widened, as did Lili's.

"How did you find out...?"

The witch laughed. "Yes, I know about that. My girl, you must have learned by now that very little stays quiet here."

The witch looked at Lili. "Our Katya is quite the progressive when it comes to shaping the minds of young ladies. I'm sure that's no surprise to you."

Lili stared at Katya before slyly smiling. "You sneak. Is that where you disappear to when you're, say, working with the guards on their archery?"

Katya rolled her eyes. "Sometimes, yes."

The blonde girl shook her head. "Still surprising me."

Katya nodded, blushing. "Yes, surprises, fine. Can we get back on the marked path, please?"

"Of course." Athena turned to Lili. "My dear, I'm going to have to talk about you for a few moments as if you're not here. I apologise."

It was now Lili's turn to blush. "I understand."

"Katya, do you think it's a coincidence that you met Lili when you did?"

Lili's blush began to creep up her ears as well as her face.

"How do you mean?"

"At the time you were the lowest in your life, you met someone who, even after you pushed her away, was willing to listen to you and appears ready to keep listening. If what you told us today didn't make her get up and leave, I can't imagine what it would take. Am I right, dear?" The question was directed at Lili.

The blush was now touching the roots of Lili's blonde hair. "Yes." Her voice was quiet yet confident. Katya sighed. "No, I suppose not. I don't believe in coincidence."

She truly didn't. She had never felt the kind of love she had for Lili with anyone else. She'd had dalliances, yes, short flings that were more about forgetting the difficulties and chaos of her chosen profession for a few hours than creating any kind of connection.

But love? It was still a concept that Katya was wrapping her head around.

Fayne chirped from her perch, finding that comment worth her approval.

Athena drained her drink and leaned forward. "Now, Katya, back to you, my dear. Please be patient with me for a few minutes as I attempt to word this in the proper fashion." She took a moment to gather her thoughts.

"You are a warrior. With your skills, there are few other words that fit. But you're a warrior with conscience, with compassion. Who has doubts, who shows resolve, and who is capable of great love.

"The sooner you start to once again see yourself not as a tool, but as a person that possesses those qualities in addition to your many unique skills, the sooner your true identity as Katya Greenleaf will become clear to you again."

Katya's tears once again began to fall. This time, however, they weren't tears of sadness or grief, but ones edged with happiness. With hope.

"However, part of being a warrior is also your deep connection to being an Oathtaker. At some point, you will have to reconcile your feelings towards the Council. I'm certain they've been keeping an eye on you as you've spent the last few months here, but at some point, they will want to know what's going to happen with one of their greatest assets."

"I suppose, yes."

"Surely it's crossed your mind?"

"It has, yes. I'm sure if I started poking into the darker corners of Fandalore, I'd find some watchful eyes that were sent here to keep track of me. At some point, I'll have to venture out to speak with the Three. They will have questions. To be honest, I have some questions of my own." Katya's voice turned cold, and the warrior at her core peeked through.

Athena cleared her throat. "Yes. Umm...at any rate, that can be discussed another time." This was an area she wasn't ready to tackle with Katya quite yet, at least not in front of visitors.

Athena leaned back in her chair. "Katya, despite this immensely important conversation today, our journey together really has just begun. Healing of this type is like…a fellenwort fruit. You peel away a layer of the hard outer skin, thinking the fruit is underneath, just to find more skin. Once you peel away enough, you get to enjoy the sweetness at the core. Yes, I quite like that description." She gestured again at her parchment, making notes for the future.

"I anticipate many more fascinating conversations with you. I believe you have the gold stashed away to keep this relationship interesting."

Jiris snorted through his cold pipe.

Athena looked at him sideways, chastising him with her gaze, before smiling and standing up. "I think I'll get some wonderful space in next year's Healers' Journal when I write up these sessions and the breakthroughs we'll make. Anonymously, of course."

Forced into silence, Jiris rolled his eyes.

The witch ignored him. "I'll have some medicines made up for you. One of them should stop the nightmares. The other will help with the feelings of panic and edginess that come over you. Make sure you tell me when you get close to finishing them. You can't stop taking them without some nasty side effects that I don't think you would appreciate."

"Thank you. I can stop here later to pick…" Again, Athena pointed to the shelf by the door, where two small bottles stood waiting, both bearing her name.

Katya turned to her, confused. "How did you…"

"Oh no. I've told you before, healer's secrets."

Jiris harrumphed. "Damn magic."

"Hush, you. Or you can leave without having any of the stew bubbling away in the kitchen."

Jiris kept grumbling under his breath, but started towards the curtained door at the back of the room.

Athena put both her hands out to Lili, who took them. "Thank you, Lili. You're a remarkable young lady. Katya is in good company between chats with me." She squeezed the girl's hands before turning to Fayne. "The same goes for you. Keep taking care of her."

Fayne chirped and whistled in reply.

"Good. I think."

She extended her arm to Katya and shook. She turned with a swish of purple robes and headed for the curtain. "Next week at this time, Katya. Please be prompt."

Halfway through the curtain, she stopped. "I hear that the captain of the guard took a job overseeing security arrangements at a new casino in Goldleaf. This town could do worse than to have you at the helm of our safety. The Town Regent is a frequent customer here. His wife prefers a certain perfume that I make, and in very small batches. I'm happy to have a chat with him."

She disappeared behind the curtain, Katya and Lili watching her depart.

Lili shook her head. "How eccentric. Even for a witch. I think." She smiled broadly. "Regardless, I like her."

Katya laughed. "That was my exact reaction as well." She tapped her shoulder and Fayne flew to her. "Come on, you two, let's get some fresh air." Elf and human walked through the market. Katya noticed that very few people crossed the street to avoid her anymore, and most were inclined to greet her.

"My, I feel like I'm walking with a celebrity."

"Yes, it's hard being so renowned. Lili, could we sit for a moment?"

Lili looked at her. "I was waiting for that. Of course."

They walked off the street into the Tacky Rat, a little out-of-the-way tavern they had taken a liking to. Since her bar brawl, Katya had become much more careful in choosing places to socialise.

They sat at a quiet table at the back, and Katya ordered two mugs of green apple ale. After the server brought the mugs and made some small shop talk with Lili, they were alone.

Katya sat quietly for a moment before speaking. "So...now you know everything. At least about what happened that day. Like Athena said, there's a lot floating around up here," — she tapped her head — "that I'm going to need to sort out."

"Yes. I'm glad I was there for it. But I'm tired after just hearing it. You must be exhausted in telling it."

"I'm drained, I won't lie."

They savoured their drinks, enjoying the crisp taste and the cool dimness of the tavern.

"Lili?"

"Yes?"

"Do you...see me differently now?"

"Well, of course. How can I not?"

She answered with such quickness that Katya assumed she was waiting for the question. "Oh." Her reply was very quiet.

Lili reached out and took Katya's free hand. "Kat, why do you assume that's a bad thing? I still respect you as much as I ever have. I find you as fascinating as

I did before, perhaps even more. I can't judge you. I have neither the right nor frame of reference to do so." She sipped at her ale. "If anything, I'm happy that it's had this impact on you."

Katya put her mug down. "Pardon?"

"It validates everything Athena said, doesn't it? You had a reaction, albeit a horrible one, to the situation. I would be much more worried, terrified, to be honest, if you had killed all those things and experienced the death of your friends and didn't have *some* reaction. Maybe that's how you were before, maybe this was a tipping point. I'm not sure. Perhaps you're not sure either."

Katya considered Lili's words. "That's incredibly open-minded."

"I think we both have to be open-minded about all this, Kat. I know there will be ups and downs, good days and bad, and I'm ready to ride them out with you. That will mean tolerating occasional moodiness and reminding you when your medicine vials are almost empty. Maybe sometimes it means holding you so tight it feels like I'll never let you go." She took another pull at her ale. "All I really know is that I find it reassuring that the elf I love has a conscience and is willing to face the deep questions she has to answer head-on. I know it won't be easy for you."

Katya heard that word again. *Love.* It was still difficult for her to reconcile.

Lili burst out laughing. "For someone who's done what you have in your life, you certainly panic at odd things. You have a terrible face for hiding matters of the heart. No wonder you had to tear up that card game. You must have an awful gambling face."

"I've been gambling for decades and I'll remind you that I won that card game on the square, thank you. Tearing it up was because of the cheating."

"Noted." Lili drank from her ale again. "And stop changing the subject. Yes, Katya Greenleaf, Oathtaker, it's love. At the age of twenty-five, Lili Fallendew, spunky tavern server, has fallen head over heels in love with an elf. Not just any elf, but a flame-haired adventurer who is as comfortable washing her clothes naked in a freezing swamp as she is teaching wide-eyed girls about the world outside the walls of Fandalore."

Katya sat without speaking, sipping her ale. "Spunky girlfriend? Is that how I should introduce you?" she finally said, a note of curiosity in her voice.

Lili smiled her wide, lovely smile. "I like the girlfriend part, but if you'd like, feisty would work too." She took Katya's other hand and looked into the elf's grey-gold eyes with her deep blue ones.

Even after months of looking into those eyes, Katya thought that part of her stomach had perhaps torn itself away from the rest and was doing cartwheels in addition to somersaults.

"I've loved you since I ran my finger over this tattoo." She turned Katya's wrist over and stroked the skin there. "Huh, I never noticed before. You can feel the lines."

"Yes. It was more like a brand than a tattoo, so it actually raised my skin a bit." Katya closed her eyes, enjoying the feeling of Lili's fingers on the sensitive skin of her wrist. When she opened her eyes again, Lili was still looking into them.

She sighed. "Damn you, Lili."

Lili raised an eyebrow. "Wasn't expecting that."

Katya laughed. "Damn you because I'm going to have to start hearing people tell me I robbed your crib. I'm over a century older than you."

Fayne, eating some dried sardines the server had brought for her, squawked with a note of reproach.

Lili looked at the bird. "What did she say?"

"She's reminding me that some things should just be taken day by day."

Lili nodded. "She's a smart bird." She thought for a moment. "In our case, it might matter, though. You'll still look almost like you do now when I'm the old crone. Maybe a few grey streaks in that beautiful red hair, but people will say you're ageing gracefully and wonder why you're with me."

Katya stroked her chin before replying. "Humans around here live to, what, a hundred or so?"

"If they take care of themselves, yes."

"Well, that gives us around eighty years. Let's make the most of it." They sat in silence for a few minutes, enjoying the lingering glow of the words.

"Kat?"

"Yes?" The alcohol was combining with the emotional hammering Katya had gone through that afternoon, making her pleasantly sleepy.

"Are you falling asleep?"

Katya laughed. "I could."

"So, for now, you're still the old crone. Good." Lili clucked her tongue in mock disapproval. "That's unfortunate. I was going to suggest that we enjoy another bath, change and then let dinner lead into another night of wine, stories and watching the sunrise."

"Hmmm. I don't know. No vampires or anything to kill during the night?"

"If it happens, I'm not too worried. No matter what else you may become, or have been, you'll never be the maiden in distress. A girl can feel safe with you."

Katya drained the rest of her ale. "You're on, young one. I need to stop at the armourer's and pick up a new bodysuit, though. I'll let you pick out the colour."

Lili sighed. "Kat…please don't take this the wrong way, but you need to expand your wardrobe. You look great in those bodysuits, and I get why you love them. Self-repairing and all that. But there are so many lovely clothes in the world. How about a bit of shopping in a store that doesn't suggest a mace as an accessory?"

Katya made an elaborate show of rolling her eyes. "Fine."

Lili smiled, her eyes lighting. "Oooo, this will be fun. Like dressing dolls when I was little." She finished her own ale and took Katya's hand. "Come on, let's go."

The elf laughed. "I love seeing you act like a girl. I'll get to live those years again through you. I was busy learning to set snares and fire my first bow in what would have been my twenties, if I was human."

"A typical childhood, huh? Were you foraging off the land or did you eat at home?"

"A bit of both. Speaking of home, wait until you see some of the elven clothiers where my family lives. Dresses that will make you look and feel like a goddess."

"Meeting your family? That's quite a step."

"They'll love you like I do. Come on, let's go spend some hard-fought coin. I'll even let you pick where we go for dinner."

"My, we're feeling generous. But if you insist…"

"I do. Then drinks and talk till we can't keep our eyes open anymore."

Lili kissed her, letting it linger, full of promise. Then she led Katya by the hand to the door of the tavern, out into the bright sunlight of what looked to be a new home for the elf and her bird.

"How about it, love?" Katya asked Fayne. "Are you ready to see another sun come up?"

She squawked a reply.

"Yes. Me too."

Glossary

Axinite: A very hard, but brittle stone used to create extremely sharp knives and medical instruments. The stone is black in colour, so much so that it has virtually no reflection. This makes it an ideal weapon for quick and quiet attacks that spring from the dark of night.

Fandalore: The city where most of Katya's story takes place. A small city in the southeast corner of Nakall, it is presided over by the Town Regent and defended by a group of guards. Fandalore is an average city, full of homes, merchants, shops, inns and the other services that both residents and travellers alike may need.

Fespyx: A relatively rare metal. It is usually found in veins that criss-cross with silver, giving it some of the powerful properties against undead creatures that pure silver possesses. Fespyx needs to be worked by more advanced blacksmiths and is usually combined with another metal when making weapons.

Goldleaf: A city a few hours travel from Nakall, noted for its substantial population of gaming houses, inns, taverns and brothels, not to mention an extremely high crime rate.

Green witch: A practitioner of magic based on a strong connection to nature. Green witches are adept at creating medicines and are extremely empathetic, making them excellent healers. Can be contrasted with their sisters who practice Black magic—summoning demons, for example—and White magic—often dismissed as parlour tricks, such as summoning then making a bird or small animal disappear.

Naga: One of the lesser-known races of Nakall. A form of large and intelligent snake with muscular arms and a long tail that is used for both weaponry and balance.

Nakall: The continent where the story takes place. Nakall is roughly rectangular in shape. The landmass is split north-south by the massive Blackwall Mountain Range and east-west by the Dalrial River—although these names may change locally in some spots, any reputable map will always label them properly. As a result, Nakall is comprised of four separate sections, each with their own unique cultures and society.

Prelium: A common metal found across Nakall. Deposits of prelium can be unearthed in any corner of the continent and it is mined by several different races, generally for use in shields and weapons. Easy to find, easy to shape and very cost-efficient for mass production.

The Scary Salmon: A popular string of taverns, known across Nakall for quick service, cold drinks, fair prices and no-nonsense security guards.

Ranger: A class of warrior once very prevalent across Nakall but now slowly disappearing. Rangers are proficient at many aspects of combat, woodcraft and warfare without specializing in any one area. They are being replaced by newer and younger warriors who tend to be highly skilled in one or two specific areas of combat.

Spoolwood: A dark-coloured and extremely dense wood. These properties make it ideal for making walking sticks, canes or fighting staffs.

Spriggan: Once thought to be extinct, spriggans are sturdy folk who could pass for humans until one notices the twigs, leaves and moss that make up their heads. While unable to speak, they are fierce fighters, and their actions speak for them. As to be expected, spriggans are not overly fond of fire.

Want to see more like this?
Here's a taster for you to enjoy!

Sanctuary: Winter Howl
Aurelia T. Evans

Excerpt

Renee took the last sip from her Samuel Adams and set the finished bottle down next to the first one. She smiled and nodded at Marie, who had come over to take the empty bottles and leave the receipt. There were no words between them. Usually Marie would chat to her customers, but she'd learned when she'd moved to Antoine five years ago that Renee Chambers would not look at her, half of the time wouldn't talk and the other half of the time would stumble through some painful attempt at conversation. Renee had got better as she'd come to know Marie, but it was still more comfortable for both of them when Renee didn't try to talk and Marie didn't try to make her.

Renee left the cash tip on the table, clenched the leash and slid out of the booth. Her legs stiffened when she saw Josh Beall and Marcus Levinson a few booths down. She had not seen them come in, and although she had heard their laughter, she hadn't recognised it as theirs. She would have to walk by them to leave. The warm body against her leg reassured her, nudged her in the right direction. She took one step, then two. Her knees loosened and let her walk. She instinctively — and fruitlessly — tried to hide in her long, light blue coat.

"...saw her at the supply store getting her checklist squared away," she heard Josh say.

"What's it been, two months since she last came down here?" Marcus asked.

"What does she do up there all alone, anyway?" Marcus asked.

"Roswell says she gets a lot of mail," Josh said. "He says she has help, but I don't believe it. She wouldn't let anyone up there. I bet she does it all herself. Completely crazy."

Renee closed her eyes and breathed in. She was not so egotistical as to believe that everyone in Antoine talked about her, but it was just her luck that she had to walk by these two rubes when they were. Neither was too far into his mug for slurred speech, but they were far enough that they couldn't gauge their volume.

"Maybe she does porn," Marcus suggested. "You know, video stuff."

Josh snorted. "Frigid bitch like her? Don't think so." He leaned forward conspiratorially. "Hey, what if we went up—?"

"Hey, Renee," Marcus said, even more loudly then they had already been speaking. Josh turned around, his scruffy but reasonably attractive face lighting up with a sly grin when he saw her huddled against the booth table behind them.

"Speak of the scared little devil," he said, raising his glass. "Want a drink? You look a little tense."

Renee's eyes darted from Josh to Marcus to Marie to the door. At another nudge to her leg, and she stepped towards the door.

"Yeah, come on, sweetie," Marcus said, misinterpreting her direction. "We'll make it worth your while."

How? Renee thought. By drooling on me and trying to feel me up with all those smooth moves you've cultivated over the last ten years? She didn't say anything, of course, just kept inching along until she finally started past the table.

She lurched forward when Marcus delivered a hearty smack to her ass. It didn't hurt, but Renee could feel her face start to burn and her chest tighten. At least she could move her legs faster now that she was past them.

"Hey, now, none of that in here," Marie called from behind the bar. "Have a good day, Renee. Don't be such a stranger."

"You always run away," Josh shouted after her.

"I wonder why," Renee muttered, her tongue looser now that she was out of the bar and no one was looking at her. "Come on, Britt, one more stop before we go home."

"Hey, Mommy, can I pet the dog?"

Renee winced at the high frequency of the voice and hoped that the mother would know the appropriate way to answer her child. No such luck.

"Hello, miss. Can my daughter pet your dog?"

Antoine was not exactly a highly populated town, but it had a fair tourist trade, particularly downtown Main Street, which was described in most tourist guidebooks as colourful, cheerful, folksy, and unique. Renee did not know about unique or folksy, but many tourists liked to come by for the ambience. And like most townies, the Antoine population had both respect for tourist dollars and frustration with the tourists themselves.

Especially when tourists did not know a service dog when they saw one.

"I'm sorry, ma'am," Renee said, emphatically not looking at the woman. That sometimes helped, and the warm feeling of Britt against her leg reassured her. "She's working."

"Oh, I'm sorry... Hey, wait, you're not blind." The overly polite apology turned into a similarly grating voice of parental annoyance. "If you didn't want Lisa to pet her, you could've just said. There's no need to lie."

"I'm not lying," Renee said. In fact, she was a terrible liar, but that was not the issue at hand. "They do more than help blind people. Please... I need to..."

"Well, that's just rude, having a dog around when you're not really blind and then not letting a little girl pet it," the mother said indignantly.

"I'm sorry. She's working." The words came out short and clipped and curt, but Renee was not really that angry. Her throat was just tightening, and she could feel her shoulders curling in.

"Bitch," the woman muttered under her breath as she grabbed her daughter's free hand—the girl's other hand had been playing with Britt's tail. The little girl was lucky that Britt was an extremely well-behaved dog. The woman led her daughter across the street.

"Good girl," Renee whispered, rubbing Britt's ear gently. "Ready to go?"

She barely had to tug the leash in the direction of the grocery store. Britt had a deep bond with Renee, had been with her most of her life and been her service dog for about five years. She could feel where Renee wanted to go.

Renee admired Britt's beauty beneath the deep green service vest. So many people confused her for a Siberian husky, and Renee understood the mistake. They were both northern sled dogs, but malamutes were bigger, with thicker fur. Britt was a little larger than average, and the darkest parts of her fur — set off by the usual white accents — were almost black. Malamutes were not traditionally service dogs. But Renee had loved Britt since the first time she'd met her, and the feeling had been mutual. There was friendship and respect between them, a connection that she had never managed to make with any of the people at school. It was really no wonder she spent all her time around dogs — she understood them and got along with them so much better than she did with most people.

With Britt in front of her, Renee felt secure in her steps. The sides of her coat hood blocked out her periphery, like blinders on a horse, and she felt a little more confident where she put her feet. Besides, with a large dog like Britt with her — a dog that was occasionally confused for a wolf — she felt more protected. Like a celebrity with a bodyguard, thankfully without the paparazzi.

They made it to the grocery store in about a ten-minute walk. That was what she liked about Main Street. Almost everything was within walking distance, so all she had to do was drive into Antoine, walk around a bit, then drive back home when she was finished, rather than drive from one place to another, and another, and another. Renee was able to stretch her legs after the long drive into town, and certainly Britt needed the exercise as well.

Renee did not need to go to the grocery store often, and she did not necessarily need to go now, which just went to show how much better she had become in public places. But she wanted to get a few treats to tide herself over before all her orders were shipped in. That was actually how she did most of her shopping — online through bulk providers. She had the space, the money and the resources, and most of the things shipped in needed to be shipped in bulk. Besides, it was such a long drive between Antoine and where she lived.

There had been a time right after her father had died when she could not even walk into a grocery store without panicking, a time when she could not walk off her property without feeling everything coming in to crush her, as if the entire world had a force field of inhospitality. That was what each successive building had felt like once she stepped out into the world — like a heavy, unpleasant curtain surrounded each of them, and it would take all her effort to pass through. And sometimes she couldn't.

About the Author

J.B. Knowles has been a lifelong lover of works of fantasy, first creating Katya and the Greenleaf family in high school as roleplaying characters.

After a long career in the fields of justice and mental health, J.B. finally had a chance to build a full world on paper for Katya and to breathe new life into adventures started over thirty years ago.

J.B. is married and has two sons and three dogs who all share an stately old farmhouse in a quiet corner of Canada.

J. B. loves to hear from readers. You can find their contact information, website details and author profile page at https://www.pride-publishing.com

Sign up for our newsletter and find out about all our romance book releases, eBook sales and promotions, sneak peeks and FREE romance books!

www.ingramcontent.com/pod-product-compliance
Lightning Source LLC
Chambersburg PA
CBHW021425200626
46814CB00015B/844